88.6% _____

Visit the Morongo Basin

Are 100% Idiots

Volume 1

BY

KENNETH B. GENTRY

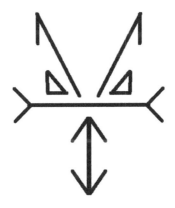

88.6% of the People Who Visit the Morongo Basin
Are 100% Idiots

Volume I

ISBN Number 9781645708001

FIRST EDITION

FIRST PRINTING

MARCH of 2o19

WRITTEN & PUBLISHED BY

KENNETH B. GENTRY

www.HighDesertVarnish.com

INTRODUCTION

I have lived and worked in the deserts of southern California for many years and strictly worked in the High Desert region for the last half of the twenty-tens. I was very fortunate to have found the Morongo Basin when I did and now I can't ever imagine leaving it. But one unfortunate part of living in such a wonderful area of the world is always having to share it with the many people who come to visit. My childhood was spent in the County of Los Angeles, so living somewhere exceptionally appealing to tourism has always been something I have been familiar with.

Recently it has become easy for everyone to see that there are more people visiting the High Desert region of southern California, especially the Morongo Basin, than ever before. Personally, I also believe that it has been equally as easy to see that the majority of the people who are visiting the Morongo Basin are not very smart. The local news frequently reports stories of tourists who have done idiotic things that outrage, depress or baffle us High Desert residents. But there is another, more subtle degree of idiocy displayed by most people who visit the deserts of southern California which isn't often highlighted by news reports and can only truly be observed if you live here year-round.

I do live here in the Morongo Basin year-round. I am no scientist, but I have done a hefty amount of research and investigating and have even performed a handful of field experiments. The results that I have come up with are staggering. Again, I will restate that I am not a scientist and I will further state that I am also not a mathematician. But it appears that the majority of the people who visit the Morongo Basin are idiots. After all the research and calculations that I have performed, I hypothesize that 88.6% of the people who visit the Morongo Basin are complete idiots.

The following collection of short stories was designed to

help illustrate this hypothesis. While these short stories were all inspired by true events which took place in the deserts of southern California, this is actually a work of fiction. I have changed the names, places, events and identifying details to help protect the privacy of individuals. So any resemblance to actual persons, living or dead, or actual events is purely coincidental.

This book was a labor of love which was mainly created to entertain those of us who call the Morongo Basin our home. But I am hopeful that it will also entertain, and possibly educate, the many people who decide to visit the Morongo Basin. I have purposely left 34 mistakes in this book for Jurgen Stephan Creed. Can you find all 34? Enjoy.

-**KENNETH B**. GENTRY

CONTENTS

CHAPTER 1
STING OF THE STOWAWAY

Mike loved his wife, Brenda, and his two young boys, James and Alex, very much. In fact, he loved all of his family and all his friends very much. But there was one thing that Mike cherished more than anything else in the whole world and that was his elaborate garden. If anyone ever described Mike, they would surely describe his love for gardening. He lived with his family in a beautiful house in Malibu, CA, and anyone who knew Mike knew about the eccentric passion that he expressed for tending to his extensive garden there.

There was a birthday party for Brenda's mother that they all planned to attend that Saturday. But Mike had woken up early that day, as he did every day, to get some more work done in his garden. Brenda's mother lived in an nice old house way out in the desert, in a place called Wonder Valley, CA. It was about a four hour drive if they didn't hit any traffic. So they had planned to leave around 9AM which would get them to her house around 2PM, after they completed a little family tradition that they always performed during long-drives to the desert. By 8:3oAM, Brenda had reminded Mike nearly ten times that he needed to eat something before they left. But Mike continued tinkering about in the back yard, tending to his garden chores and plotting out a plan for his new trees.

In addition to the plethora of different types of plants and trees that skirted Mike's backyard, there were three new apple trees that he had just planted near the back of his house which he planned to skirt with large rocks. As a family tradition, every time that Mike's family would visit their relatives out in the desert, they would take an extra hour or so to drive off the beaten path and pick up a bunch of rocks for Mike's garden. But no one really took the tradition quite as seriously as Mike did. He loved the careful art of mixing different trees, plants, soils and rocks with other embellishments to make a unique and perfectly harmonized garden. In fact, there was something in his backyard from every trip he had ever taken with his family.

In preparation, he had already cleared the area that he wanted to border with rocks that morning. But he and had then started his everyday garden chores when he should have been getting himself ready. Brenda brought Mike a glass of apple juice and made him drink it down in front of her while he finished up watering a table covered in potted plants. She then took the glass from him and put a small breakfast sandwich in his hands before reminding him that they needed to leave in fifteen minutes and she wanted to make sure that he ate something before the long drive. Mike finally finished up outside and hurried into the house to finish getting himself ready as his sons were already loading the family's large leisure travel van.

When Mike was done getting himself ready for the long day ahead of him, he grabbed his keys before everyone jumped inside the van. Mike backed out of their long driveway, threw the van into drive and they headed off towards the freeway. For a Saturday morning, the traffic was light as anyone could have wished for and they made great time. Mike eventually got over into a carpool lane and they coasted along for a couple hours before they'd left the city and were headed up to the High Desert. Mike drove them up through Morongo Valley, then Yucca Valley and on through Joshua Tree.

They really had made great time, as they found themselves entering Twentynine Palms just before 1PM. Mike drove along

2

Highway 62 until he spotted an area off in the distance that interested him. He turned on the nearest crossroad they came by and took the van down a long dusty dirt road towards some rocky looking mountains. After driving past a handful of small houses, the road got a bit narrow and desolate looking. But soon they were far from the main highway and parked at the foothills of a large rocky mountain. Everyone got out of the large van and grabbed some heavy work gloves from a pair of buckets that Mike had brought along.

James and Alex went around filling the buckets with smaller rocks that they thought looked interesting while Mike and Brenda loaded the back of the family van with larger specimens. They piled and piled rocks into that van for almost a full hour before they were all ready to go to Brenda's mother's house and start celebrating. But when Mike spotted one last large rock that he wanted to take, their plans quickly changed. When Mike went to remove the large rock from underneath a little dead and fallen Joshua Tree, he was amazed to find that the entire dead tree actually weighed significantly less than the large rock.

The Joshua Tree that laid before Mike had once stood at least twice his height and consisted of a slender main trunk and two short arms which both narrowly branched off midway and extended upwards, parallel with the trunk. He had seen a million of the dead trees across the desert, but had always assumed that they all weighed as much as any other heavy fallen tree did; even one as slender and narrow as the one which had particularly struck his fancy that day. The plan had originally been to collect a bunch of rocks for Mike's garden. But as he looked at that little fallen Joshua Tree, images of it sitting at the foot of the three new apple trees in his garden flashed before Mike's eyes.

Mike quickly abandoned the rock that had brought him to that site and made Brenda help him carefully drag the tree carcass to the van. There, the whole family tried to help as Mike pushed and then pulled the dead Joshua Tree onto the top of their van. It took a little while for him to strap it down securely to the roof, but once he had it secured, they all jumped inside the van and headed back down the dusty dirt road towards Brenda's mother's house. After driving down the dusty dirt road, Mike turned back onto the highway.

Shortly afterwards just as they made the turn off of the highway onto the old dirt road that went to the birthday girl's house, they were pulled over by a California Highway Patrol officer. Mike knew that he hadn't been speeding and had properly used his turn signal. So the whole family was pretty curious why they had been pulled over so very close to their destination. The officer explained to them all that they had actually committed a federal crime by taking the Joshua Tree that was strapped to the top of their van, as the Joshua Tree's removal or destruction is both federally and state prohibited.

They were pretty lucky that the officer had better things to do and simply made them dump the Joshua Tree on the side of the road. If their van had been inspected, the officer would have probably had some questions about the rocks for them. Mike got out and removed the straps before James and Alex helped him slide the big Joshua Tree off the top of their van and onto the side of the little dirt road before the CHP officer wished them well and headed off down the highway. Mike was a little upset as they all got back into the van and headed off towards Brenda's mother's house.

Once they got to the house, just under half an hour late, Brenda's mother came out and grabbed both of her grandchildren, hugged them tight and kissed each of their foreheads before greeting Brenda and Mike. Once inside, they met a bunch of other family and ate a bunch of food. Sooner than later, Mike had all but forgotten about the incident with the highway officer. But when Brenda's mother was talking to a handful of people and mentioned that Mike and Brenda had arrived a little late, someone joked that it had to have been because they had stopped to pick up rocks for Mike's garden. That prompted Mike to speak up and mention the Joshua Tree incident to the whole family.

He explained how amazing the dead tree was, how brilliant

4

it would have looked in his garden and how upset he was that the CHP officer had made him get rid of it. Everyone took his story with a slightly different response. For the most part, everyone understood where he was coming from. But some of his family did give Mike a little grief for having taken the federally protected tree. Especially since he had planned to park the van with a stolen Joshua Tree strapped onto the roof right in front of the house, where all the neighbors would see it plain as day. But the birthday girl quickly cooled the situation down by changing the subject all together and telling everyone that she wanted to open her presents.

The rest of the day went without a hitch. Brenda's mother enjoyed all of her presents and the huge chocolate cake that followed shortly there after. There was good food enjoyed by all and a few bottles of good wine shared by most of the adults. The weather couldn't have been nicer, so everyone spent a great deal of time out on the back patio. But as the early evening came, everyone started heading home and eventually Mike, Brenda and the kids had to leave themselves. Brenda's mother gave James and Alex both a big, strong hug before she kissed each of their foreheads, hugged Brenda and Mike and said goodbye to them all.

One their way down the dirt road towards the highway, Mike just couldn't help himself. He hadn't bought the huge cargo sized luxury van that they were all driving in just so he could haul his family and some rocks around. They could have comfortably fit a pair of kayaks in addition to his whole family inside that massive van if he wanted to. Mike wanted that Joshua Tree. He wanted it for his garden and he simply couldn't think of anything other than the vivid image of the dead tree resting in his garden at the foot of his three new apple trees. To his family's surprise, Mike pulled over to the side of the dirt road where the officer had made them dump the Joshua Tree.

He then instructed his sons to help him move some of the rocks out of the back of the van. Brenda didn't give much protest, as she was a little confused about what they were doing. But when Mike instructed James and Alex to help him

5

move the dead Joshua Tree into their van, Brenda got out of the front seat and started questioning Mike. As they slid the long, light and slender dead Joshua Tree bottom-end-first into the van, Mike explained that they had only been caught because the tree had been right out in plain sight and that no one would be able to see what they were hauling inside the van.

Much to Brenda's protest, they were able to get the Joshua Tree into the van. They sat the odd looking stump in between the two front seats and laid the trunk and two slender branches on top of the back two rows of seats, where James and Alex would have to sit awkwardly divided by branches. It fit with very little wiggle room and it made a horrible mess of the entire van, as well as Mike, James and Alex. But Mike's passion for decorating his garden was a hard force to reckon with and he assured Brenda that he would have the van professionally washed the very next day.

They crammed into the van, Joshua Tree and all, without attracting any attention and headed back onto the highway. As they drove home, every bump that the van went over would cause the dead Joshua Tree to shake loose little bits of dirt and rocks that fell all over the van. The big rocks that they had collected bounced together and rumbled loudly from the back of the van the whole drive. Brenda and her sons would have been mad, if they weren't so amused at the crazy eccentric lengths which Mike was willing to go to in order to decorate his garden.

Any animosity Brenda had quickly passed and eventually they were all laughing together at how loud the rocks were and how filthy the van would be by the time they got home. But as they passed through Los Angeles County, Mike suddenly stopped laughing and very randomly slowed the van way down and pulled over to the side of the freeway as quickly as he could. Brenda grabbed his shoulder as he pulled over and begged him to know what was wrong. Mike, suddenly speaking very slowing, told her that he felt like he couldn't breathe properly and his right arm was in severe pain.

Brenda called 911 as James and Alex panicked in the back

6

seat while their father slumped over and passed out in front of them. It was almost ten minutes, ten grueling minutes which seemed to stretch out forever, until emergency responses arrived at the scene. Paramedics quickly addressed Mike while firefighters took Brenda and the kids out of the car and far from the side of the road to safety. After the emergency response crew had a few minutes to investigate the situation, they reported to Brenda that Mike had been bitten by a bark scorpion on his right shoulder.

Bark scorpions are found throughout much of Arizona but are rather rare in California and only live in the southeastern portion of the golden State. They happen to have the most toxic sting of all the scorpions in the United States and Mike had passed out after his throat swelled up from being bitten so close to his neck. They took Mike to a nearby hospital in an ambulance but they also removed the Joshua Tree from the filthy van before they let Brenda drive it to the hospital. Mike later made a full recovery. But he also received a very expensive fine for having removed a Joshua Tree from its home.

CHAPTER 2

"LOOK WITH YOUR EYES, NOT YOUR HANDS." SAID THE BLIND PARENTS TO THEIR DEAF SON

It had been a very long flight. Luca and Nina Neth, along with their four year old son, Max, their five year old son, Matteo, and their six year old daughter Melissa, had traveled to Southern California all the way from Trimbach, Switzerland. There, they met up with their old college friends Fredric and Marta, who had also been visiting California from Switzerland that summer with their little four year old daughter, Beth, and their five year old son, Liam.

Luca, Nina, Fredric and Marta had all visited the Palm Springs area together about ten years earlier and had wanted to revisit the area again ever since they'd left that first time. The nine of them all met up in Los Angeles at a car rental lot next to the airport after the Neth's long flight finally landed. There in the parking lot, they hugged and kissed and celebrated being able to see each other. After Luca rented a van, the Neths followed their friends as they headed south on a congested freeway through some of the world famous Los Angeles traffic for a few tedious hours. After a long and busy drive, they finally arrived at Desert Hot Springs early in the evening.

Luca followed Fredric off the freeway and through the little town where they stopped at a grocery market and all got out to stretch their legs. They had rented a couple rooms at a fancy spa hotel nearby for a few days, so they stocked up on snacks, drinks and other random supplies at the grocery store before they headed to their hotel. Luca again followed Fredric as they drove to the fancy spa hotel. There, they all checked in and unloaded their luggage. They'd booked two suites next door to each other, one for each family, that had a door which privately connected the pair of suites.

It was hot out in the parking lot and by the time everything was unloaded, Luca and Nina, already jet lagged, were exhausted. Max, Matteo and Melissa weren't quite as tired as they already knew Beth and Liam and enjoyed spending time with them. Not wanting to cook anything fancy, they prepared and ate a small, random little dinner of potato salad, cold cut sandwiches with hot macaroni and cheese. When they were all done eating, the kids quickly grew just as tired as the adults had been. They called it a night and all went to sleep.

They each woke early the next day and enjoyed a big breakfast at the hotel. They all ate nice hefty servings, as the restaurant there at the the hotel didn't serve anything small. After breakfast, they took the kids out to have some fun and to check out the area they were staying in. They drove around exploring Desert Hot Springs before they headed across the freeway into Palm Springs and visited the Aerial Tram. The kids were each shocked and amazed, hyper and jumping, when they boarded the tramcar and lifted up into the air while climbing up the face of the mountain. At the top of the mountain, they spent a good while inside the lodge checking out the museum-like displays and amazing mountaintop views.

The amazing atmosphere and the ride up the mountain had energized the kids and the five of them began to gain speed and run in every direction. When Nina and Marta took little Beth to the bathroom, Luca and Fredric tried to catch up with each other, but weren't able to, as their kids loudly bounced all around, like balls in a pinball machine. In an attempt to keep them all in one spot, Luca took all the kids into the gift shop.

There, the kids continued to swarm around like a tornado. But as long as Luca and Fredric stood at the entrance to the shop, he knew where all the kids were and could finally get a chance to talk with Fredric.

Nina and Marta returned from the bathrooms with Beth and helped to wrangle all the kids back into order. They entered the shop and ordered each of their kids to drop the random items that they'd been playing with and had wanted to buy. When the children all protested, Nina bribed them by asking them if they wanted to go outside and see the top of the mountain. When the kids all jumped at the opportunity to explore more, Nina told them they'd come back after they went outside. As the kids finally started to comply and drop the random souvenirs they'd pawed, Marta apologized to the lady running the shop for the mess that they'd made while Nina herded them outside.

The two families spent hours playing and exploring outside. After the kids had finally grown tired from running and playing, they all headed back into the lodge and ate a big dinner at the restaurant. By the time they'd finished their meal that evening, the gift shop was closed. The kids were all very upset that they wouldn't be able to get any of the random trinkets they'd wanted. But as the sun was setting, so too was their energy level. They appeased the kids with a simple white lie, saying that they'd all come back later and visit the gift shop when it was open again.

They all boarded the tram and rode down the face of the mountain. Unlike the ride up, the kids weren't hyper and jumping around. Unfortunately the parents were just as tired as the kids were and when they reached the bottom of the mountain, they quickly shuffled to their cars and returned to the hotel in Desert Hot Springs. It wasn't another hour before they were all fast asleep. They'd had a nice, long, active and fun day, which is why they all slept so well that night.

Everyone woke early again the following morning and enjoyed another large breakfast at the restaurant in the hotel. That day they drove up the highway to Joshua Tree National

Park and visited numerous desert attractions under the hot summer sun. Plenty of sunscreen and water was passed around that day. Although Luca, Nina, Fredric and Marta all enjoyed the majestic desert wonderland, their kids all grew bored with the whole place within the first hour. By the end of that hot summer day, the children were each ready to explode with boredom.

The following morning they enjoyed what they had dubbed their "traditional breakfast" at the restaurant inside the fancy spa hotel in Desert Hot Springs. The children were a little restless that morning, but their parents assured them that they'd enjoy themselves more that day than they had the day before. After breakfast, they all jumped into their rental cars and headed up the highway to Yucca Valley. There they visited a natural history museum which had many different exhibits for both adults and for children.

Visiting the museum seemed to energize the children just like ascending the mountain on the tram ride had energized them the day before. They began to bounce around instead of walking, their voices grew louder and louder with each bounce they made and they started to grab and touch anything any everything in their site. As the four parents enjoyed a little reminiscing about their previous trip out to the desert so many years prior, Nina periodically broke from the conversation and tried to quiet the kids down.

"This is a museum you guys." Nina tried to tell them all in a quiet voice, using an exceptionally calm tone. "We have to be quiet in here, or we'll upset the animals and they'll kick us all out."

The children all heard only one word that Nina said. "Animals?" they all immediately responded back to her.

With that, she directed them to an exhibit which housed a few local bugs and animals. This didn't quite the kids down any. But as the kids all grouped around the animals, their loud talking, sticky little fingers and random bouncing about was at least centered into one corner of the museum. The parents took full advantage of this and enjoyed looking at some of the local

12

historical exhibits for a while. They knew that their little Melissa always looked after her younger brothers and Liam always took care of his little sister.

They eventually left the museum and grabbed some lunch at a barbecue restaurant off the main highway that they'd seen the day before. It was a dimly lit western themed saloon with a huge bar, loud rock and roll music playing and a never-fading aroma of smoked meats throughout. They quickly realized that t wasn't a great place to take a bunch of kids. But the food smelled so amazing that they had to try it out. The parents seated all the little ones at the end of a big table and used a few booster-seats for the youngest of them. As was expected, the kids started to get pretty antsy and bored in the dark saloon, up until the the food arrived.

Everyone enjoyed sharing some amazing barbecued ribs for a sticky but delicious lunch before they headed back out to explore more of the desert. They parked at a few different places along the main highway where they could easily walk to a handful of little second hand shops and art studios. Each time they entered a shop, one of the parents would inevitably end up having to tell all of the kids something like "don't touch, just look" or "look with your eyes, not with your hands." None of the kids ever paid them any attention and constantly picked things up, moved things around and touched everything they could reach.

The four parents tried to enjoy their time together or to shop for themselves. But one of them would always eventually end up having to tell the little ones to stop what they were doing or to drop what they were holding. Eventually they passed through a shop that sold cold drinks and snacks. At this location, the poor shop keeper looked on in disbelief as the kids grabbed and crunched bags of chips and candy as their oblivious parents admired jewelry all the way on the opposite side of the shop. Eager to appease the kids, Luca bought them all bags of candy and sodas when he purchased a pair of ear rings that Nina wanted.

Each child then held a bag of candy and a cold drink, which

they all consumed as they were dragged from one store to another. This kept the kids quiet until the snacks started to run out. When they entered a funky little shop in Old Town Yucca Valley, little Matteo immediately saw a shopkeeper stocking little bags of blue candy. When he demanded that his parents get him some of the candy, they quickly denied him, reminding the little guy that they'd just bought him sweets and he still had a soda in his hand. This angered Matteo, who began thrashing about the shop with the other kids as they had in every other store.

As the four parents talked near some natural minerals that were displayed near the entrance of the little shop, the kids took their time checking out things all throughout the building. No one saw when little Matteo took a look behind one of the shop's display shelves. There, scattered on the floor under the shelf that was right in front of him, were a handful of little blue bits of something. Remembering how his parents had angered him when they denied him the blue candies, Matteo scooped up a handful of the little blue treasures and put them in his pocket. He would enjoy some more candy whether his parents said he could or not.

But the day was beginning to come to an end as the sun started to descend and inched its way behind the many mountains surrounding Yucca Valley. There were still so many shops that the parents all wanted to visit before they had to call it a day. They'd wanted to shop a lot that day and then eat a big dinner before bed, as they'd be leaving for another Southern California destination early the following morning. So they began dragging the kids through stores at double speed. Each parent was just a little less observant than they already had been for the duration of the afternoon, as they truly wanted to see as much of the Morongo Basin as they could.

No one saw Matteo eventually grab a handful of that blue candy looking treasures from his pocket and pop them in his mouth. They sure didn't taste like what he'd thought they would taste like! They were bitter and the texture wasn't right; it tasted like it belonged on the floor. Matteo swashed the nasty

14

mess down with the rest of his soda before setting the empty soda can on a store counter, much like he would set empty drinks down on the kitchen counter at home. His family had already left the shop that he was in a few minutes earlier, so he finished up investigating the last few things he found interesting in the little store, before hurrying out the door to catch up with his parents.

They stopped at a dozen more art studios and random shops that evening, before the sun finally set and they headed back to the spa hotel in Desert Hot Springs. There, they all unloaded their purchases from the long day of shopping and relaxed in their rooms for a short while, before heading to the hotel restaurant. When it had come time to eat the big dinner they'd planned for, they all found themselves sad to admit that they'd have to miss their traditional breakfast at that restaurant the following morning. So they decided to have their final meal in the Morongo Basin there, at the hotel restaurant.

The restaurant was packed that night and it ended up being a long wait for their meals to arrive at their table. But when it finally came, everyone at the table was famished and ate like animals. Everyone, except Matteo. Matteo ate a little bit of the chicken Fettuccine Alfredo that he'd ordered and then quickly lost his appetite. He sat around quietly for a while as his family ate but eventually got very tired and started to fall asleep at the table. His parents were enjoying a chance to talk with Fredric and Marta about their plans for the next day.

It wasn't until Matteo just about fell face-first into his pasta dish that his parents noticed how odd he was acting. When he became unresponsive at the table, they initially thought that he might be choking. But, as Luca and Nina both rushed to his side, Matteo began throwing up profusely over himself and the table. Both Luca and Nina began to panic as they both noted that their son's vomit was a strange blue color. Fredric and Marta both tried to keep the children from freaking out as other people in the restaurant began to come to their parent's side to try and help poor unresponsive Matteo.

An ambulance was called, the rest of the Neth family's

plans were canceled and eventually a huge lawsuit was filed against the spa hotel. It was discovered at the hospital that Matteo had eaten rat poison, causing him to experience convulsions at the dinner table and turning his vomit the red-flag poison indicating blue color. The long lawsuit that followed ended in the spa hotel restaurant's favor, as they had never experienced a rat problem and had never purchased or used any rat poison. Not like the small desert shop that sold candy did.

Matteo had seen the store clerk restocking candy at that small desert shop because they had an infestation and rodents had eaten up their candy inventory the day before. They'd spread out rat poison behind and under their display shelves to try and stop the infestation. Unfortunately, even though the public trail eventually went in the restaurant's favor, no one ever discovered where Matteo actually got the poison that he'd ingested. Furthermore, no one ever truly questioned Luca and Nina's parenting. The spa hotel eventually recovered from the negative publicity. But Luca and Nina's parenting skills, having never been questioned or criticized, never improved.

CHAPTER 3
PARTY FAVOR FOR A DESERT RAVER

Walter was forty-one years old and that winter he was getting ready to host the biggest party that he had every thrown in his entire life. He enjoyed raving and had been passionate about throwing elaborate house parties since he was in High school. He'd hosted parties at his parents' huge house in Rancho Cucamonga, at various friends' houses and at a few random venues throughout the Inland Empire which he'd rented out. But this time he had some really big plans. Walter had rented a big house near the heart of Pioneertown, just a couple hours drive from his hometown, where he was going to host the biggest party that he, or any of his friends, had ever seen.

It was a bit of a long drive for anyone coming from Rancho Cucamonga. But everyone who Walter had invited to the party had already been to Pioneertown before to see different bands play at the bar in town and had enjoyed themselves every time they'd went up there. Walter had saved for months to be able to afford the fancy rental house and all the essential items he would need in order to make this the best party anyone had ever seen. He had promoted it for just as many months so that he could get as many people to RSVP as possible. The online short-term rental service that Walter booked the posh rental with had advertised that the house could accommodate large parties and he was going to make sure that he took full advantage of that fact.

Walter packed his suitcase and a bunch of heavy music equipment into his prized red sports car, left the flat-lands that he called home and got up to the rental house in Pioneertown early the day before the party. He worked best when he was alone, so he had made sure to give himself the better part of a day to start getting things ready for the big event. He briefly met up with a rental agent at the front gate who gave Walter a key to the house and a clicker for the gate. It was cold out that day, so the agent quickly welcomed Walter to the town and asked that he leave the key and gate clicker in a small lockbox there at the gate when he was ready to check out. The agent then thanked Walter before leaving him to enjoy the property.

Walter opened the gate and pulled his fancy red sports car all the way up to front of the large house before he went about inspecting the grounds. The house was surrounded by a big, flat dirt yard that had been scraped bare of anything but a few Joshua Trees and was bordered by a tall wood fence, except the front of the property, which hosted an equally tall chain link fence. From the outside, the property looked rather minimal and a little too modern for the rustic Western atmosphere of the neighborhood. But Walter found the inside to be grand and extensively modernized throughout. He unloaded his suitcase and the heavy music equipment from his car and started getting the house ready for the epic party that would commence the following evening.

The first thing that Walter setup was his extensive music system so that he could listen to some good beats as he got things ready for the party. Unlike a traditional house, this one didn't have many dividing walls and was designed mainly to accommodate a bunch of people in one grand room which was attached to the kitchen and a large covered patio. It was stuffy in the there and Walter tried to turn on the air. But, as it was the middle of winter, the swamp coolers were all covered and disconnected from their power sources. So Walter went around

18

and opened a bunch of windows to help air out the house.

In addition to a few bathrooms scattered around, he found the two private master bedrooms far in the back of the house as he went around cracking open windows and letting in some cool air. But Walter didn't end up using either of those bedrooms until much later that night. He stayed up into the very early hours of the morning listening to music and getting everything ready for the big party. Walter then woke up early the next morning and quickly showered and dressed before he made a pot of coffee in the big fancy kitchen.

He enjoyed a hot cup of dark roast in the massive grand room while he stared out the big windows and enjoyed the beautiful desert view all around him on that cold desert morning. A little while later there was a knock at the front door. He hadn't been expecting any of his friends to start showing up for a few more hours. But he wasn't expecting anyone else and figured that most of his friends were probably eager to get the party started already. So, thinking it was an early party guest of his, Walter flung the door open with a loud "Hello, hello!"

He was a little started to find and older gray haired gentleman man standing there in the cold. The man was very polite and introduced himself as Walter's "neighbor from down the way." He explained to Walter that he lived a good handful of lots away from the rental house and was able to hear the music that Walter had played all the day and late into the night before. The old man said that he honestly thought it was really great music, but asked that Walter please keep the volume down so he didn't spook any of the many horses who lived around there or bother any of the people who lived nearby.

This wasn't what Walter wanted to hear that morning. He had been planning this party for too long and he had paid way too much for this rental to care what anyone thought about his music. So Walter told the old man what he thought he'd would want to hear. Walter apologized, said that he would try to keep the noise down and neglected to mention that he expected nearly a hundred party guests later that evening. The old man thanked him and commented on Walter's fancy red sports car parked out front before he said goodbye and headed back out the gate which Walter had left open the day before.

Later that day, one by one, Walter's friends all arrived at the fancy rental house and the big and once empty yard soon housed dozens of parked cars. Walter hung out with everyone throughout the day, but when the sun began to set, tons of other friends began to show up and soon the yard was a massive parking lot filled with cars randomly parked in no particular order. There wasn't an exact time the party started that night. But by the sun had set that winter evening, the music was bumping and the grand room was filled with people dancing and drinking.

As the party went on through the night, more and more people arrived, the music got louder and the house got hotter and stuffier. At one point that night, Walter went around the house and cracked most of the windows open a little more to try and compensate for how hot and stuffy the place had become with all those guest. Letting in just a little bit of the cold winter air instantly made a world of difference throughout the whole house and the rest of the evening was spent comfortably dancing, drinking and enjoying the party. That night went just as Walter had planned it. The music was great, tons of people showed up, everyone partied hard and good memories were made.

By the next morning, the rental property looked like a bomb had gone off inside it. The majority of the guests had been smart enough not to drink and drive and had spent the night there instead. Mike had slept in one of the master bedrooms with a special lady friend of his, eight random people had slept in the second bedroom and a handful of guests had all slept in various areas of the grand room. Once the sun was high in the sky, they all woke up and drank coffee together while they recollected about the awesome party the night before. Everyone moved slowly as they tried to ignore their hangovers, but Walter's friends were all very nice about helping him clean up most of the mess leftover from the night before.

Eventually the house looked less like an explosion had gone

off and Walter's friends all began to leave in small groups. One of Walter's friends had arranged to borrow most the heavy music equipment for another upcoming party. Once that friend had left, the majority of the heavy stuff was gone which made things a lot easier for Walter to organize and pack before he would be able to head home. Soon, the last friends left and Walter packed up the rest of the things that he had brought for the party. He took one last walk through the house to make sure that he hadn't forgotten anything before he loaded up the trunk and passenger side of his fancy red sports car. Walter locked up the house and took one final walk around the outside of the property to make sure that no one had left anything in the newly wheel-torn dirt yard which had served as the parking lot the night before.

Once he was sure that he had the property as good as it was going to look and that no one had forgotten anything, Walter headed to his fancy red car with a smile on his face. That party had been exactly what he wanted and anyone who attended would surely remember it forever. But Walter's smile shot right off his face when he approached the driver's side of his car. His jaw fell wide open and his eyes bugged out in disbelief as he focused on the door of his prized red sports car. There, etched into the side of Walter's expensive car, in big paint scratched letters, were the words "Thanks For The Great Music!"

CHAPTER 4
READY. SET. FLOW!

Lately, it seemed like work had been getting harder and harder for Tim, Tommy and Trent. They all worked together at the same construction company and lived near each other in a little neighborhood on the outskirts of Las Vegas, NV. Each of them was married with children, was pushing forty and was generally a hardworking man. They had all become fast friends almost a decade earlier, when they stated working together at the construction company. Over the years, the three of them had taken a handful of trips together; sometimes with all their families and sometimes just the three of them.

Years ago, they had learned that all three of them shared a taste for gold prospecting. Since making that discovery, they'd all made it a point to try and go out looking for gold together at least a couple times a year. All three of their fathers had enjoyed prospecting for gold well before them and they could each remember their fathers taking them out to teach them where and how to look for gold at a very young age. They all enjoyed traveling with their families. But they had planned their next trip just for the three of them.

They headed south towards California that Tuesday morning in Tommy's SUV which they had loaded with plenty of water, ice chests filled with cold drinks and food, camping supplies, gold prospecting equipment and snacks for the long drive. All three of them were members of a gold prospecting association that allowed members to camp and prospect on numerous mineral claims that they owned across the golden State. Their plan was to camp out at one of the association's claims for a few days and return that Friday night. The claim they chose was near the Old Dale District, an hour or two north of Palm Springs in the High Desert.

Unfortunately, right before they'd left, the weather reports began indicating that it would rain that Thursday, right where they had planned to camp, and would probably continue raining through the end of the weekend. But that area hadn't seen much actual rain in the past few years, as the majority of storms there tended to pass through rather quickly. So none of them paid much attention to the reports of rain. They all hoped that they'd be able to prospect the area for a few dry days before any storm came through. In fact, if it did end up raining while they were there, the water might end up helping them find gold a little easier. And if it really ended up raining, they would just head home early.

They had actually all previously been to the Dale District to prospect with their fathers on separate occasions, back when they were little kids. But the only thing either of them could clearly remember about the area was that it was in the middle of the desert and the only way to get there was on a really long dirt road across a deep desert valley. After a few hours of driving on the freeway, the three of them finally made it onto Highway 62, where they eventually passed through the towns of Joshua Tree and then Twentynine Palms. Shortly after driving through Twentynine Palms, they followed their directions off the highway and onto a dirt trail that they lead up and into the foothills beyond.

The dirt trail seemed to go on forever as it swayed left and right through what looked like an enormous wash. As they drove along the bumpy trail and into a deep rocky valley, it quickly became clear that this was the old road that they all remembered from their previous trips out to the area. They didn't need to travel through that valley for too much longer before they had reached the area that they'd marked off on their maps. Tommy parked the SUV in a spot off the trail next to a handful of large Creosote bushes and the three of them went about putting together their camp site. The walls of the valley they found themselves in consisted mainly of large dark red rocks while the valley floor was mainly light colored sand peppered with dark green plants and bushes.

After they'd unpacked their equipment and set up their tents, the three of them explored the valley for the rest of the day. The area looked like it would be good gold bearing land and the actual mineral claim that they were on was filled with spots that they wanted to dig. But as the day soon came to an end, they instead retired to their camp where they built a big fire and enjoyed a nice dinner. The stars were bright that night and everyone stayed up well after dinner and talked around the warm fire. They all woke early the next morning, ate a quick breakfast and headed out to some of those nearby sights they had wanted to dig the day before.

It wasn't even 1oAM in the morning and the temperature must have been in the high eighties. The weather reporters had to have been crazy, because that morning, Tim, Tommy and Trent were all sweating profusely under clear blue skies. They had perfected working together as a team to prospect for gold many years earlier and worked through that area as efficiently as they could. Trent would use a shovel or similar tool to dig up dirt into buckets from a spot that they all liked while Tim would use a handful of classifying screens and a drywasher to concentrate the dirt from the buckets. While they were doing that, Tommy would pan out the concentrates in water.

If Tommy found color, or gold, in his pan, he'd tell Trent to continue digging where they'd found it. As efficiently as they worked and as well prepared as they were for desert weather, the heat made it incredibly hard for them to get much done without having to constantly brake for water. But they were finding little bits and flakes of gold here and there. So they kept working along, enjoying their time away from work. Fortunately, a cool breeze finally blew threw the valley as they worked and helped beat the heat of the day.

Early in the afternoon, the three tired friends all returned to their campsite to have a well deserved lunch and to look at the bounty that they'd accumulated so far that day. The sandwiches they ate helped re-energize them. But, more than anything else, it was the small vial filled with almost a gram of placer gold which made them all want to head back out and keep working. Additionally, that really was the only full day they had to spend there. So after eating, hydrating and resting a little, the three of them headed back out to the spot they'd stopped prospecting earlier and got back to working it.

Shortly after they got back into the rhythm of working, it was Trent who first noticed and pointed out to the others that there were big dark clouds slowly creeping over them. But they were still finding little bits and flakes of gold, so they kept on working along. As those clouds slowly blew in over them, the humidity got higher and higher and the cool breeze that had once helped them beat the heat eventually slowed to a stop. All three of them were positive that it would rain the following day, but each one of them seemed to refuse to look up. They had found a sweet spot and the little bits and flakes of gold they found were starting to fill up that vial mighty quick.

It wasn't until Tommy couldn't continue to see well enough that they had to stop working and address the situation looming overhead. By then, there were a couple more hours of light left in the day, although the sun was long gone behind a thick layer of clouds. But they hadn't seen a single drop of rain fall so far. They had, however, found a few grams of gold in just a half a day's work. So Tommy stopped panning and helped Tim concentrate material which they then bucketed to pan out later, while Trent continued digging in the spot where they'd had the best luck that day.

They kept working well into the evening and only stopped when it got too dark for any of them to see just about anything that they were doing. Each of them carried their tools and equipment back to the campsite. There, Trent made a fire and started to get something ready for dinner while Tim and Tommy went and carried the twelve heavy buckets of concentrates they'd collected back to the campsite. Finally, everyone ate and rested by their camp fire. It had been a mighty hard day's work and, although the sun had been gone for hours by then, the temperature was still somewhere in the high seventies.

After eating and resting for a while, the three friends looked at everything that they had found that day. As it turned out, that evening they actually needed two vials to contain all the gold that they had worked so hard to find. They were each ecstatic and exhausted at the same time. It was quite a good amount of gold for three people to have found on the first full day of a prospecting vacation. Unfortunately for them, it was also the last full day that they had to look for more. So they decided that they'd try and work as much as they could the next day before they had to head back home and, if they ended up finding as much gold as they already had, they might even decide to stay a little longer.

Everyone went to sleep thinking about gold that night. They had found well over a gram each and they had only worked the source for a handful of hours. Plus, they'd really only brought amateur prospecting equipment. If they put in more time and had better equipment, who knew what they might be able to dig out of there. Between the high humidity, the warm temperature and the weight of the hard day's work they had all put in, the three of them all ended up falling fast asleep and resting heavily through the rest of the night. They slept so well, in fact, that none of them woke up when it started raining early that morning, just before sunrise. It was almost two hours before they woke up to a very wet, dark and gloomy looking morning.

As soon as they were awake and out of their tents, they knew that they would be in big trouble if they didn't leave really soon. Sheets of rain fell steadily as random white flashes of lightning lit up the sky above the valley they'd camped in. That little storm that was suppose to roll through was right on top of them and the trail that they had driven on to get there was already flowing with a couple inches of fast moving brown water. Their dreams of finding more gold would all have to wait. They took down their tents, packed up their things and loaded everything, including the dozen heavy buckets of concentrates, into the SUV as quickly as they possibly could.

While they loaded the SUV, the rain fell so hard that not a single thing was spared from being soaked. The temperature was back to the high eighties, so as wet as everything was, it wasn't cold in the slightest. That was the only thing which went in their favor that morning. Tommy jumped in the SUV and turned it on just as a loud crash of thunder echoed through the valley like a bomb had gone off above them. As soon as Tim and Trent were inside themselves, Tommy flipped on the windshield wipers, threw it in reverse and hit the gas. But the SUV didn't go anywhere.

They were already stuck. So Tim and Trent both got out as quickly as they could and ran to the front of the car as the rain fell harder and harder all around them. The sky kept alive with white flashes of lightning while they gave the SUV a good push from the front so Tommy could back it up. Tim and Trent both jumped in as the SUV puttered backwards and into the heavily flowing stream that had actually been the trail before they went to sleep the night before. Tommy threw it back into drive and headed towards the paved highway miles away.

The long dirt trail that they had taken to get out there just days before had now become a large mass of brown flowing water, easily half as deep as the tires on their SUV. There wasn't any trail or perfectly clear path to be seen, so Tommy just pointed the truck in the direction where he thought the trail would have been. He mainly just kept driving forward as fast as he could without hitting any of the trees or large rocks along the valley floor. As they grew closer and closer to the end of the valley, it seemed like the water rose an inch every minute. By then, the SUV swerved from left to right, barely going the direction that Tommy pointed it as he sped towards paved, safer roads.

While Tommy drove the SUV through the speeding brown

torrent that surrounded them, the water actually rose up and over the hood of the car for a bit. Fortunately for them, the water level then began to drop faster than it had risen as they finally neared the face of the long valley. Once they'd made it out, the water that they sped through was only half a foot deep. But an incredibly loud crash of thunder roared out from behind the speeding SUV. It was so loud that it made all three of them simultaneously duck and quickly look behind them. As they turned back towards the direction that they were headed, the last thing they saw was a large rock, dead ahead of them. If you thought that thunder was loud - you should have heard how loud that crash was.

CHAPTER 5
SHOCKED BY MY HEARTS, CAUSE THEY MADE ME LATE

The Mcstay family had been looking forward to a birthday party at the park all summer long. Every year they celebrated their kids birthdays in the big water park way up at the Whitewater Preserve. Sandra's birthday came first each year in September and the whole family always made the drive up to Whitewater to celebrate it with her. That year Sandra was going to turn ten years old and her birthday fell on a Saturday. That meant that in addition to everyone in her family who planned to come and celebrate with her, Sandra also got to invite a handful of her classmates to come along too.

When the big day finally arrived, Sandra's parents filled up the back of their car with picnic foods, a cooler full of ice and cold drinks and a bunch of presents for the birthday girl. They filled up the trunk with beach towels, water toys, squirt guns and anything else that they thought the kids might enjoy playing in the water with while they would be up there. While Sandra was getting ready in her bedroom and wasn't around to see, her parents and younger brother also packed up a cake and five big pink hart-shaped Mylar balloons on long red chords, which they hid far in the back underneath a large blanket.

It was a long drive to Whitewater from Orange County,

31

where the Mcstays lived. So the whole family was up and ready to go by 9AM. They left on time and followed a little family tradition of theirs by swinging by a fast-food restaurant before they got onto the freeway. Whenever the family was about to get on the freeway for a long drive and they had to leave early, they'd each enjoy an egg sandwich and some hash browns on the road. For the kids it was a fun treat and for the parents, who each enjoyed a coffee as well, their true delight came with knowing that their kids would end up falling asleep shortly after they finished the greasy eggs and potatoes.

The "long drive" for Sandra and her little brother translated into countless hours of exhausting driving along endless boring highways while listening to their parents talk about things that kids could care less about. In actuality, the drive wasn't really all too long. They made it to Whitewater in well under three hours, including the stop for fast-food on the way. The freeways had been amazingly clear for a beautiful Saturday morning in the summertime. But Sandra and her little brother couldn't hack it. They had both fallen asleep shortly after they finished their egg sandwiches, well before they passed through Banning.

Sandra's parents woke them up shortly after they got off the freeway and were heading up Whitewater Canyon. With rejuvenated amounts of energy, Sandra and her younger brother burst awake with excitement. The freeways all looked the same. But they both knew exactly what the short drive up Whitewater Canyon looked like. With every minute that passed from this point further, they knew exactly how much longer it would take until they arrived at the Whitewater Preserve. Sandra had eagerly been looking forward to this birthday all year. Her level of excitement was both physical and audible. By the time that they were able to park in the shady parking lot, both kids were feverishly clutching their door handles, fit and ready to burst out of the car.

That is exactly how it happened. As her father was putting the car into park, Sandra and her brother both had their doors open and were jumping out. "Hold it!" her mother quickly yelled.

Both kids stood at their doors while their parents gathered their things and got out. They had purposely parked right in between the shady picnic area and the area where kids could play in the running water. Sandra's mother then took Sandra and her brother to the trunk and grabbed a bunch of towels and water toys before she walked them over to play in the water. Sandra's father unloaded the rest of the car and set up food and drinks at one picnic table and birthday presents at another. He laid a pink table cloth down over the center of the table where the presents all went.

When it came time to display the big pink hart shaped balloons, Mr. Mcstay took them to the present table and began untying them from the small metal ring they were all attached to and individually tying their long red chords to the boards which made up the corners of the picnic table. As he would tie one down, he'd put a present on top of the knotted cord to make everything look extra special for his little girl. But before he could finish tying down the third balloon, his own parents drove up into the parking lot and parked next to his car. Waving to them, he quickly picked up the biggest present, a bright neon pink box, and put the remaining three unsecured balloon chords under it, which kept them in place just fine.

Mr. Mcstay ran over and happily greeted his parents. While he was helping them unload their car, more family and friends soon began to arrive. Before too long, the parking lot was more than half full and everyone that Sandra had invited had arrived. By 1PM that afternoon, there were heaps of Sandra's friends and family celebrating in the shade, playing in the water park area or walking around enjoying the preserve's beautifully landscaped grounds. The summer afternoon couldn't have been nicer. The sun was bright and hot, but there was a very soft breeze that cut the heat and there were tall shady trees which shaded the majority of the grassy park.

The conditions were perfect for playing in the water and the kids only began to tire of the aqua frolics after a couple hours of nonstop play. By 3PM, Sandra had just one thing on her mind: presents! Well, maybe two things: presents and food! The smell of barbecued hamburgers and hot dogs that had been wafting through the air had finally got to Sandra. When she left the water to dry off, the majority of her friends and family followed along shortly after her. Halfway across the parking lot Sandra's jaw dropped open when she saw what had been setup for her in the picnic area while she had been playing in the water.

There was a table with a pink table cloth completely covered with presents, most of them wrapped in pink and purple. There were even big pink hart-shaped balloons! Her father was barbecuing and talking with a bunch of other adults in the shady area by the tables when she headed in his direction. As Sandra approached all her party guests, she was bombarded by a bunch of people who hadn't been able to hug or kiss the birthday girl yet that day. When the long line of guests had finally all wished her a happy birthday and the countless hugs and kisses were finally all through, Sandra got herself some good looking food.

The hot dog Sandra ate was good, but the cheeseburger she enjoyed right afterwards was delicious. Her family and friends all ate just as much as she did. There were chips and dips, a handful of different types of salad and even a bunch of different fruit that someone had cut up. If there was room left in Sandra for cake, she surely didn't know where it was. But as full as she found her belly to be, that cool summer breeze gently blew the smell of the desert landscape past her and put a smile on her face. This was exactly how she had wanted to spend her tenth birthday and before she knew it, she had a cake in front of her and everyone was singing happy birthday to her.

After Sandra blew out the candles and everyone cheered in celebration, the party goers all ate cake with ice cream and drank milk. Everyone was just as cleanly as they were merry. The more and more food that was consumed, the more plates and napkins, soda cans, beer bottles and plastic cups the metal trash can closest to the party consumed. It was nearing 4PM, and while the sun wasn't going to be setting anytime soon, everyone did have a long drive to get back home ahead of them.

There were no complaints from Sandra when her parents suggested that she start opening her presents shortly after everyone had enjoyed cake and ice cream.

Even though she was exhausted from playing in the water and eating so much food, Sandra started ripping into her presents like a tornado. She was amazed with how many people had been so thoughtful and she was very thankful for each and every present, no matter how big or small it was. Although extremely grateful, she was as graceful as a Tasmanian Devil while she shredded through presets as fast as her mother could hand them to her. When her mother picked up a big neon pink box, three of the big pink Mylar heart spaded balloons went flying up into the air. She grasped for the long red chords, but wasn't able to get to them in time.

As the big pink hearts floated up above the party, a handful of voices were heard from the guests. One of the balloons got caught half way up one of the tall trees which shaded the party. But the pair of balloons that were still tied to the small metal ring they came on caught that slight breeze and were quickly carried up and over the trees and into the bright summer sky. Everything from "Wow!" to "No!" was unanimous shouted for about two seconds before everyone returned their focus back to the birthday girl. Sandra herself displayed a big frowny face as she watched the balloons get away from her mother, but quickly returned to a happy smile as she began to open the large neon pink present that was handed to her.

After all her presents were opened, Sandra went about thanking everyone for having helped to make all of her birthday wishes come true. She had really had a great time that day. While the adults talked and enjoyed the afternoon breeze as it picked up just a bit, most of the kids played with balls in the shaded grass. A few of them did return to play in the water park area. But the breeze made playing in the water just a little too cold to enjoy as much as they had earlier that day. It wasn't too much longer before most of the guest started to pack up and head home.

Sandra's parents took a few minutes to clean up anything

that was left over from the party and all the trash cans in the park area were filled by the time the were ready to leave. After Sandra's grandparents hugged her tight, they got into their car and waived goodbye to everyone as they drove off. Sandra, her parents and her little brother were all exhausted. They packed up the rest of Sandras presents and the leftover food before they too got into their car and headed home.

As Sandra's father drove down Whitewater Canyon towards the freeway that would take them all to their home, Sandra smiled to herself. Her birthday really did go exactly how she had wanted it to go and she couldn't have been happier. Sandra and her little brother also couldn't have been any sleepier than they already were as they started home. Shortly after they got onto the freeway, well before they passed through Banning, both Sandra and her brother fell fast asleep while the sun started to set around them.

When they woke up a few hours later, they were both shocked to see that they were still on the freeway. By now, the sun had long set and the evening would have been dark if it weren't for the thousands of red brake lights that filled the freeway all around them. As Sandra rubbed her eyes she realized that she knew exactly where they were on the freeway. They hadn't even made it half way home yet. Even if the freeway was completely empty, it would still take her father more than an hour to get them all the way home from where they were currently sitting in traffic.

It was a very long, hot, quite and boring drive the rest of the way home. They spent the rest of the trip driving from zero to fifteen miles per hour, with hundreds of cars crammed around them in every direction. Every direction, except the opposite direction the Mcstay family happened to be headed. The opposing traffic seemed to whiz by at a hundred miles an hour. Both Sandra and her brother had slept a long while and they had again both woke up with a bunch of energy. But that energy was to be a curse, which only kept them awake and attentive as their car crept along.

The Mcstays finally made it back to their house just before

midnight that night. By that time it was hard for Sandra to tell if she was hungrier than she was tired. But she was too hot to care. This time, as her father put the car into park and turned it off, no one had their hands on their door handles. Everyone fell out of the car like a bunch of zombies and then shuffled into the garage door. No one talked very much. Everyone just set their things down inside the cool, air conditioned house and went about doing what they needed to do before they could all go to bed.

Sandra took her presents inside and her little brother brought their toys into the garage while their parents unloaded the heavier things from the car. Her mother took the leftover food into the kitchen where shed used a remote on the counter to turn on the television in the living room before she started putting things into the fridge. Sandra, her brother and her father all got everything inside the house and closed up the garage behind them. Shortly afterwards, Sandra and her brother were both in their bedrooms and her parents were both in the kitchen when everyone in the house heard a breaking news story about that traffic they'd just driven through being reported on the television. As each one of them heard the reporter talking, they quickly made their way into the living room where they all silently watched the breaking news report together.

The reporter was standing on a bridge over the freeway that the Mcstays had just been on while tons of cars were still slowly creeping along in bumper to bumper traffic below him. The reporter mentioned tons of traffic for miles and thousands of houses without electric for the past few hours. Apparently, earlier that evening, a pair of large pink hart-shaped Mylar balloons had blown into a set of power-lines and blew a transformer that then knocked out the power for a couple miles in every direction. Shortly after that, there had then been a fatal car crash when a driver didn't realize that the traffic lights were all running on emergency power.

The late driver didn't brake as they had approached an intersection where other cars had already stopped in front of them. They had then swerved at the last second to try and avoid hitting the stopped cars and ended up rolling their car off the road and down a short hill onto the freeway below. When they landed in the second lane of traffic, they were hit and instantly killed by another car driving along the freeway at over sixty miles an hour. The news reporter grimly announced that the pair of Mylar balloons had been directly responsible for one death, three major injuries and thousands of dollars in property damage for the electric company, in addition to thousands of people being left without electricity that a hot summer evening.

CHAPTER 6
ALL AIR TRAFFIC IS STRICTLY PROHIBITED

John and his wife, Carla, enjoyed living in the Bay Area of California. They had always loved the ocean but they also both shared an equal love for taking weekends vacations. That's a big reason why they enjoyed living near the middle of California; all they had to do was jump on the freeway for a few hours in any direction and they would find themselves in whatever kind of exotic, fun place they could think of. John and Carla tried to take advantage of every three day weekend by getting away somewhere that they hadn't been before or at least going somewhere that they hadn't been to for a long time.

Memorial day was coming up at the end of May and they had both scheduled the day off from work months in advance. Their plan that holiday weekend was to drive down to Pipes Canyon, CA that Friday night after they got off work. They had rented a nice little cabin that was in the middle of nowhere, about two miles off Pipes Canyon Road, where they would stay from Friday night until Monday morning. Then they'd leave the High Desert and enjoy a little bit of Palm Springs shopping before they had to turn north and head back home.

Thursday evening before Memorial Day weekend, both John and Carla packed up their suitcases. Thankfully the weather was suppose to be ideal that whole weekend, so they didn't need to pack up any heavy warm clothes. Maybe just a little extra sunscreen, just in case. In addition to her clothes and toiletries, Carla packed a couple of their favorite board games for them to play together while they were up at the cabin. After getting all of his clothes and supplies ready, John also packed up his video game console and the fancy new and expensive drone that he had purchased earlier that year but hadn't had a chance to fly yet.

When Friday morning came, they both woke with an excitement that was quickly put on the back burner. Sadly, for them both, they had to go to work before they could actually get on the road for their holiday weekend getaway. That being said, the couple went about getting themselves ready for work and headed off. By that afternoon, they were both antsy as could be. They met up at their house after work, tossed their things into John's fancy new yellow lifted truck and headed off to Pipes Canyon. After a few hours on the freeway and then another on the highway, they began to see large rock formations glowing in the moonlight along both sides of the road.

When they arrived at their cabin, they were both impressed and tired. The sun had set a couple hours before they arrived, but the renter knew they were coming and had left motion sensor lights on for them outside and left a lamp turned on for them in the living room. John and Carla both loved the place. There was a huge kitchen and living room, complete with a big flat screen TV and even a working old jukebox. The neighborhood, as much as they could tell in the dark, was isolated and quiet as ever. Much to their surprise, they found a few cold beers and a handful of freshly baked muffins inside the refrigerator. They were both very pleased. But, as nice as everything was, they weren't going to be able to enjoy it as tired as they were.

The sleepy couple called it a night and got themselves to bed. They were pleased to find that the California King sized bed was even more comfortable than their bed at home. It was downright luxuriousness. They slept like logs that night, both having fallen asleep just minutes after their heads hit their pillows. The following morning came and the bright sun that began shining through the bedroom windows ended up being the couple's alarm clock. After they woke, John and Carla enjoyed the muffins for breakfast. It looked like a beautiful day, so they decided to take a walk around the neighborhood and get a better sense of where they were staying.

When they had come in the night before, it had looked like they were absolutely isolated as they drove off the main highway. With the sun shining bright, they quickly realized that wasn't quite the case. There had to be at least a dozen houses on the block they found themselves on. All the houses were spaced out quite well and hidden among the many large boulders that neatly decorated the area. Carla wanted to take a drive so they could see more of the neighborhood. So the couple headed back to the house where they jumped into John's truck and drove back out in no particular direction. As they drove around, they realized that the entire valley was actually filled with houses.

Again, the structures were all very well spread out and hidden among the many magnificent natural land features. They took just about every turn without thinking twice about it. They really didn't have a plan or a direction in mind as their goal was just to see what was around them. As it turned out, the only other things that were around, besides the many large granite boulders and Joshua Trees, were more houses. Both John and Carla hadn't realized that so many people actually lived around that part of the desert. There wasn't even cell phone service once you got off the main highway.

The whole time that they'd been making plans to stay there, they had been excited about being able to stay in "the middle of nowhere." While it turned out that it wasn't quite as isolated as they had expected, it truly was beautiful. The many houses that they drove around both impressed and inspired them. Some houses had fences up that bordered off acres of property in every direction and some of the houses were really small and looked quite a lot older than others. Every now and then, they would see a house that looked more like a mansion and appeared like it was newer than John's new truck.

After they had driven around the neighborhood for a good couple of hours, the muffins that they had eaten earlier quickly became less than enough to tide them over. They turned around, headed down the main road, and drove themselves down to Yucca Valley. There they found a nice and cheap little diner, right off the main highway, where they enjoyed a nice lunch and talked about what they wanted to do for the rest of the day. Carla wanted to explore more of Yucca Valley and maybe Joshua Tree, while John wanted to go back to the house up in Pipes Canyon and relax for the rest of the day.

They had often butted heads about what they would do on the first full day of weekend getaways. Sensing an easily avoidable conflict, John quickly suggested that they finish that day off doing what Carla wanted to do. He highlighted that earlier that morning, she had wanted to take the drive that they had just enjoyed. Carla could do whatever she wanted to do that day, all day, and John would choose what to do all day on Sunday. That worked for Carla. So when they were both done with their meals, they drove around Yucca Valley visiting the many thrift shops.

Then they drove further down towards Joshua Tree and enjoyed looking at the many interesting shops and art studios. By that time, the sun was getting ready to set and they were feeling hungry again. John and Carla enjoyed a nice barbecue dinner at a rustic, cowboy saloon styled restaurant they had found in Joshua Tree before they headed back to their rental. Once there, Carla said that she wanted to play one of the board games that she had brought along. John, still full from their meal and tired from the long day of exploring, was a little hesitant. He looked really tired and he reminded Carla that he had done all of the driving that day.

Carla wasn't quite as tired as he was, but she decided that they didn't need to stay up playing board games all night for them to enjoy themselves together. After all, it was getting rather late. John took a shower and Carla read a short science fiction novel she'd brought along while resting on the bed. As she read, her thoughts wondered a bit. She started thinking about sharing that big luxurious California King sized bed with John. When he was done with his shower and out of the bathroom, Carla went to take a shower, herself. As she did, her thoughts again quickly focused around getting to spend the rest of the night together with John, as soon as she could.

When she finished her shower, Carla dried off and slipped into something a little extra pretty that she had brought along mainly just to show John. With her mind set on enjoying the rest of the evening with John, she exited the bathroom in a bit of a pose, but found the bedroom empty. That didn't slow her down a beat. She was going to show of for her man. She walked right out of the bedroom and took the same stylish pose at the face of the bedroom door as she had when she'd first exited the bathroom. But this time, Carla did end up missing a beat.

John was sitting in the living room, playing his video games on the big flat screen TV. When Carla went to go sit with him on the couch, he didn't even notice that she was dressed to impress him and wanted his attention. When she spoke up and noted that he had been too tired to play a board game earlier but didn't seem too tired to play video games now, John was still too focused on his game to pay her any attention. She grew fed up with him almost instantly and spent the rest of the evening reading her book. A couple of hours later they were both tired and went to bed. Carla was upset that they hadn't spent that night together, especially on the day that she was suppose to get to do what she wanted. But she was too tired to protest.

The next morning they both awoke again to the morning sun shining through their bedroom windows and warming up their bed. It was a bright and beautiful morning and they both woke with a good deal of energy. There weren't anymore muffins left, so they decided that they were going to head down to Yucca Valley and grab breakfast. As it was John's day to choose what to do, they made plans to leave from Yucca Valley to head up into Landers, where John wanted to visit a place called Giant Rock. They headed down to breakfast and enjoyed eating at the same little cafe that they had gone to the day before.

From there, the couple headed up Old Woman Springs Highway and into Landers. Carla had no idea what Giant Rock would actually turn out to be, as John had only briefly explained what it was to her earlier that morning. He had read about it before they left for the trip and it seemed like the ideal spot for him to test-fly his new drone. And indeed it would have been. The site stood a good distance from any houses and private property. Even after saying the name numerous times on their way up, they weren't prepared for what they found and were both shocked when they reached their destination in John's big yellow truck.

The boulder that stood before them truly was enormous, in every sense of the word. A huge chunk of the rock had fallen off to one side of the boulder; yet it still remained gigantic in stature. It was hard for John to imagine, let alone describe to Carla, that Giant Rock had once been the site of a small airport, complete with a diner. It was even harder for them to believe that years earlier a German desert dweller named Frank had dug a home out underneath the huge boulder and lived down there. The site was truly amazing and they both spent their time there pondering a million questions they had about the giant boulder.

Unfortunately for John, as grand and magnificent as Giant Rock was, that day it was also host to a great deal of wind. It wasn't worth trying to fly his new drone in that kind of weather as it was a very expensive newer model and it had cost him a very pretty penny. John was an excellent drone pilot. But even with his skills and the models advanced features, the wind made it impossible to launch. Nevertheless, John and Carla ended up spending a good deal of time there. The wind might have prohibited John from flying the small craft, but it wouldn't stop them from walking around the area and admiring the over-sized monstrous beauty that lay before them.

After exploring the site, the two of them decided they

wanted to explore more of the area they had found near their rental. They had enjoyed looking at everything around Pipes Canyon the day before, but there was a great deal of land that they weren't able to get anywhere near. Furthermore, Pipes Canyon was exactly that: a deep canyon. The area was surrounded by tall mountains on one side and black flattop buttes on the other, which, at least the day before, had kept the majority of those strong desert winds from sweeping through the area.

The drive from Giant Rock back to Pipes Canyon wasn't very long at all. They were both pleased to see that Pipes wasn't experiencing as much wind. But, as they drove down the main road, it was pretty clear that John still wouldn't be able to fly that drone anywhere around there. To be able to fly a drone safely, especially for the first time, the weather really needed to be calm and there was still just enough wind to call off the flight. Again, John was a great drone pilot. But it'd be silly to take out something so expensive when he knew that he would immediately be compensating for the wind instead of getting to inspect the drone model's fancy new features. But this didn't stop the couple from continuing to explore the beautiful area.

They drove through Pipes Canyon and turned onto Rimrock Road before investigating that fun little neighborhood. At the end of Rimrock, they found that the main road went unpaved. John might not have been able to fly his new drone that day, but surely he would be able to enjoy the off roading features that his big yellow truck offered. They continued along the bumpy unpaved road, once again not really pointed in any particular direction. John and Carla were both shocked to see how many houses there were as they drove back towards the middle of nowhere. A hand-painted sign that they passed told them that the road had changed from Rimrock to Burns Canyon. Every time they turned a corner they were able to spot houses hidden around the mountains and foothills.

Just like in Pipes Canyon, Burns Canyon had a good deal of private residences that ranged from old looking, small little shacks, to grand sized, newer constructions. But the further back they went into Burns Canyon, the less houses they saw. Eventually they were in an area that was covered in tons of tall Joshua Trees. It was a beautiful and awe inspiring sight. Although they wanted to continue exploring the area, the sun had already begun to set behind the tall mountains. John and Carla decided to call it a day and headed down to town for dinner before they went back to their rental.

That night Carla got to spend a little extra time with John as he ended up being far too tired to play video games. They slept very well that evening and awoke again the next morning when the sunshine found its way onto their bed. They were both a little sad that they had to leave that day. But they got their things together and locked up the rental before heading down to grab some breakfast. From the second they had stepped outside, John was eager to fly his drone. The weather was perfect that day. There wasn't any wind at all.

Their plan that day had been to leave from Yucca Valley and then to hang out down in Palm Springs before they headed back home. But John now wanted to stay and fly his drone instead and Carla didn't mind, as they would get more time to drive around back in the mountains they had enjoyed so much. They headed back up Pioneertown Road, passed Rimrock, and continued up through Burns Canyon. Their new plan was to get as far back there as they could, to where they hadn't been able to get to the day before. John was then going to fly his drone for a little while before they would go back down to the freeway and head home.

The drive was just as beautiful and bumpy as is had been before. That day they had a limited amount of time, so John drove took each twist and turn that the road offered just a little faster. Once they had driven a good distance past the last of the fences and houses that they could see, John turned off the main road and followed a trail off the beaten path, towards the edge of the valley. The trail was extremely bumpy and even as John slowed down, his truck was still shaking and rattling like a paint mixer. Carla and John both cracked up laughing as they looked over at each other as best as they could while rattling and shaking along.

Neither one of them had seen the wood sign at the corner where they had turned off the main road; the sign posted nearly five feet high, which clearly read "Private Road. No Trespassing." in big black letters. As they drove down the bumpy dirt road, bouncing along and laughing to themselves, neither John nor Carla saw the second wood sign that clearly stated in big black lettering, "Private Property. Trespassers Will Be Shot!" But what did catch John's focus a few hundred yards later, once they'd neared some Joshua Tree covered foothills, was a great spot to park.

When the engine was turned off and they opened their doors it was like they had walked into another world. There was no wind at all. For that matter, there was no noise at all. Just the sounds of silence, wilderness and wonder. They found the spot where John wanted fly. Carla walked around and took some pictures of the beautiful spot while John set up the drone. It didn't take very long and in almost no time at all, John had launched the drone and was testing out its handling. It was a bit louder than his previous model, but it seemed to handle beautifully.

John shot the drone straight up about fifteen yards or so, until it was higher than all the Joshua Trees, then started directing it in every direction that came to mind. As it whizzed around above them, John was able to see the view from the drone on his cell phone screen. The sight from above was absolutely amazing. The Joshua Trees looked like they were green fireworks scattered across the desert floor. It looked like they might of actually been parked on a driveway, as John was able to spot a little house hidden in the tall Joshuas, maybe two miles down the trail from where they parked.

The battery signal on his screen began to flash, so John flew the drone back to his truck where he landed it and turned everything off. He had an extra battery charged and replaced it as he called Carla over. John wanted her to get a chance to see the view from up above the treeline. Holding the screen at an angle so Carla could see it at his side, John flew the drone back

47

up into the air and started whizzing around again. The view, though miniaturized through the small screen, was absolutely beautiful.

John and Carla both stared intensely at the screen, while he turned the drone in the direction of the little structure that he'd seen before. Interested in showing Carla the potential house, John flew the drone in that direction. As they watched the screen, Carla let out a giddy laugh which was simultaneously accompanied by a large cracking noise in the distance. In an instant, the drone's feed went completely blank and the screen indicated that the drone was turned off. The couple's jaws both dropped as they looked up and quickly focused off in the distance to see the drone fall from the sky and through the treeline, maybe a quarter of a mile ahead of them.

Without thinking, John gave sprint down the trail towards the scene of the crash and Carla followed quickly along after him. It wasn't hard for them to spot the fallen drone that laid ahead, as it sat crumbled into many bits and pieces just to the side of the Joshua Tree lined trail. As John approached the pile of fallen drone, he stood over it in awe and finally took a second to assess the situation. When Carla caught up to him, John was a little confused and angry.

All but ignoring Carla, John stepped past the drone and started walking down the trail. "I think someone shot it down." he said over his shoulder.

"What?" Carla asked, as she ran to be by his side. "Are you sure it didn't just crash?"

"They are made to survive a fall like that." John said, as they walked further down the dirt trail towards a clearing in the thick shady Joshua Trees where the trail widened. "Either the battery exploded or someone shot it down. That thing was brand new!"

Clutching John's shoulder, Carla pulled hard, stopping him and forcing him to address her. "If it was shot down, are you sure it's a good idea that we should try to find the person who shot it?" she asked him.

As they reached the point where the trail got wider and the

trees cleared up a bit, there was another loud cracking noise in the distance, quickly followed by a second. Not half a second later, two clumps of dirt atop the trail instantly turned into dust directly in front of John and Carla. The couple stopped in their tracks and Carla grabbed John as hard as she could. They stood there for a few seconds, completely shocked, staring like deer in the headlights. When John took a couple of slow and cautious steps further with Carla still clinching at his side, they were both sent cowering to the ground when a third crack thundered through the desert. A third clump of dirt, this one a couple feet closer to them, went flying up into the air in a puff of dust.

Carla's grip on John was tight before, but the third shot got the message through to her. She pulled with all her might and all but started running back towards the truck with John's shoulder in her hands. John didn't give any protest and turned around with her in a flash before they both sprinted back down the trail. They ran straight past John's shattered drone and didn't slow down until they had reached the truck. They were both inside in an instant. John threw it into gear and did a three-way turn in record time before they were headed back out the dirt trail in a hurry.

As they turned around and sped along the trail kicking up a dust cloud behind them, Carla grabbed her cell phone from her purse. The main road was right in front of them and she knew exactly how soon she would have cell service again. But somehow, even though they hadn't seen them on their way in, John and Carla saw both big wood signs on their way out. John didn't slow down much, but he did stop gassing the truck down the trail as they passed the big black letters which clearly said "Trespassers Will Be Shot!" and "Private Road."

They didn't say anything for a while; not until they made it back to the main highway. Carla put her cell phone back away as John turned onto the main road. It was clear that they shouldn't have made that turn and should have probably been more observant in the first place. The dirt road eventually turned paved once again and the couple headed back to their home. Their weekend getaway hadn't been all bad. They had enjoyed their rental and some great food and shopping in town. But John and Carla both agreed that the next time they found themselves out in the middle of nowhere, they would try to stay on the paved roads.

CHAPTER 7
SNOW BLIND

The Giuseppe family was fed up with being stuck inside because of the poor weather. There weren't too many rainy days in southern California. But the last week had been nothing but rainy days and the rain still hadn't stopped. When it was apparent that everyone was getting a little stir crazy from being stuck inside, the Giuseppes all decided that they would brave driving through the rain down in Riverside and then through the cold up in the High Desert. They were going to visit the desert in the winter time.

There had been a lot of snow that winter season; something that you don't see in southern California, especially the desert, too often. The whole time that it had been raining down where the Giuseppes lived, it had been snowing up above in the mountains. The snow level had dropped that day and there wasn't just snow falling in the mountains anymore. It was falling all throughout the High Desert too. Mark and Cathy hadn't had a chance to take their kids out to the snow since they were all babies, so they were just as excited to head up the snowy mountains as the kids were.

They loaded their five year old Mitchel and seven year old Lora up into the family van, along with a bunch of extra warm clothes and a cheap plastic sled they'd had in the garage forever.

Then they hit the road. The rain kept everyone on the roads and freeways moving a little slower than normal. But they made good time skirting the foothills and making their way up to the High Desert. When they reached Banning, the kids grew very excited as there was a clear view through the rain of the snow covered mountains above. Then, while they drove up Highway 62 through Morongo Valley, the rain turned to hail and by the time they got up to Yucca Valley the hail had turned into snow. As they started heading north, up Pioneertown Road, the snow got thicker and thicker.

It didn't look like the snow was going to get any better than what they saw as they drove up through Water Canyon. There must have been two feet of glowing white snow atop everything once they finally reached Pioneertown. Mitchel and Lora hadn't ever been in snow that thick before and they couldn't wait to get out of the van. So when they finally were able to turn into the parking lot of a restaurant they all liked up there, the kids were both so excited that they already had their seat-belts off and their sweaters and gloves on.

But the parking lot was complete chaos. There were a bunch of cars already parked in there and none of them were parked in designated parking spaces. The parking lots were normally unmarked, level, dirt lots. But that day they were either a thick three feet of fresh white snow, or, in areas that had already been driven over, they were ugly, thick brown slushy messes. People had just parked wherever they pleased; if not because they couldn't imagine backing their cars up through the slushy ice and mud, then because they were so excited that the simply forgot how to operate their cars.

Mark Giuseppe was just as excited as his wife and children were. He pulled up as close as he could to the car that had turned into the parking lot ahead of him and as soon as that car used its brakes, the red lights in Mark's eyes was his cue to throw on his own brakes, put the car into park and turn it off. They were there and it was time to play in the snow! As soon as Mark parked the car his wife and children were all already jumping out of their car doors. The car in front of them had parked just a few yards ahead of them and that family was already heading for the snow atop the empty part of the parking lot that hadn't been driven over yet.

Cathy had been taking pictures with her cell phone during the drive there, but she had also brought a nice digital camera along as well. They all left their cell phones in the car, as they knew there was a good chance that they could easily be broken or get wet in the snow. Mark grabbed the old sled and Cathy took her camera before they locked the car. Cathy started taking pictures of the family right away. They all wanted a little more privacy than the parking lot had to offer, so they decided they would walk down the road just a little further where they could play in one of the empty lots in between the houses. The snow was pretty thick along the side of the road where they all chose to walk in a single file. The thick snow was hard to walk through, but it was easier than trying to walk where cars had already driven, as that ugly brown slushy mess was very slippery.

Once they had trekked a good distance behind the restaurant, they turned off the road and started walking into what they remembered as being an empty lot. There were some houses nearby, but the Giuseppes made sure they didn't cross any signs or go over any fences. The kids hadn't stopped laughing and yelling since they had left the car. As they walked along, the kids both threw snow balls and kicked at the snow with every other step they took. The whole family was amazed at how white and cold the desert had become and Cathy must of taken three pictures every two minutes that they walked.

When they had walked far enough that they could hardly hear the other family's children playing anymore, Mark tossed the plastic sled that he'd carried behind him, he bent down and rose back up with a snowball that he quickly threw at Cathy. As it burst over the hood of her sweater, she started laughing and with that, the kids simply couldn't walk any further. They started jumping around and throwing more snow balls of their own. Mark and Cathy held hands and watched as their kids went crazy in the thick white mess that was still falling just as hard as it had been when they got there. Mitchel made a snow angel as best as he could and Lora tried to make a snowman, but wasn't able to get much more than a small ball of snow to stick together.

The area they had chosen to play in didn't exactly have an incline nearby. The snow had piled up a lot higher around bushes and the tall Joshua Trees and this offered the smallest little mounds of fresh white snow. Mitchel tried a few times to use the plastic sled on these little mounds, but gave up rather quickly as it was clear that there wasn't any momentum to be found. They all continued to enjoy watching the falling snow together for a bit before the kids started to run around again and Cathy started taking more pictures.

Everything was as fun as could be; the extreme cold being the one exception. Even with gloves and boots on, everyone's fingers were starting to get numb. Cathy was taking pictures of Mitchel as he ran around with his sister when she noticed him stop quickly and bend over in distress.

"My leg is burning, mama!" he yelled out.

"Did you get snow into your boots?" Cathy asked, as she continued taking pictures.

Mark and Cathy both began walking towards their kids while still admiring just how much snow had fallen since they had parked. It was a complete winter wonderland there. And the last time they had all been in Pioneertown, they had camped in a pop-up tent and they'd even left it open when they slept because it had been so hot out.

"It *really* burns, mom. It's not snow!" yelled Mitchel in what quickly turned from a yell into an ongoing cry.

Mark and Cathy started to run through the snow to their kids. Cathy pocketed her camera and grabbed her boy. "Where does it hurt?" she asked, as Mark and Lora both got to Mitchel's side.

"My leg. My ankle. My ankle is on fire, mom!" yelled Mitchel, while grabbing at his right leg.

Cathy laid the boy down with his head in Mark's lap and started to pull up the wet jeans around his right ankle. As she rolled up the jeans, Cathy saw a few little spots of red blood on

Mitchel's white sock. But, to her shock and horror, Cathy's focus was quickly directed past the blood to a handful of thin white pins stuck in his wet sock. The boy yelled out as she rolled a little more of the cold wet jeans back. Lora grabbed her father and buried her face in his shoulder as her brother jerked and screamed.

The next roll of Mitchel's jeans unveiled a cluster of long white needles, inside the jeans themselves, inside the boy's wet sock and inside the flesh of his calf, including the back of his knee. As he writhed in pain, Cathy realized that her little boy was covered in cactus needles. She was covered in cactus needles too. As she looked up into Mark's eyes, Lora still burying her face in his shoulder, Cathy saw that Lora's jeans were also covered in cactus needles. Cathy's eyes grew wide as she focused on the small mounds of snow that stood up from the ground all around them. She peered around until she could see one of the mounds with less snow on one side of it. It was a Cholla cactus. There were Cholla Cactus all around them.

Mitchel was crying out loud now. Mark stood up and picked up his boy, doing the best he could to comfort the injured kid as he swiftly scooped him up. Cathy grabbed Lora's hand and the four of them started back towards their car as quickly as they could. As soon as they started moving fast, Lora burst into tears. It wasn't very long before she started complaining about her legs burning. Then her hands. Poor Mitchel screamed and cried the entire time they trekked back along the side of the road. This time, as they walked through the snow, with each step that they took, they were able to see Cholla cactus in every direction. There were cactus all over the place. Every place except for the road and the parking lots. Just like they had been when the family had been there the last time. What the hell had they all been thinking?

By the time they finally reached their car, the only Giuseppe who wasn't crying out loud was Mark. Cathy was a sobbing mess, Mitchel was screaming at the top of his lungs and Lora was holding her hands in front of her face with tears running down from her eyes. They needed to get into their car

55

and get their kids to a hospital right away. Other people had stopped in their tracks and stared at the family, wondering if there was anything they could do to help them. But all they saw was a family screaming as they ran and jumped into their car.

Mark and Cathy hadn't wanted to say anything out loud on the way back, but both parents knew that there were far too many cactus needles stuck inside poor Mitchel for them to take out all on their own. The boy needed medical attention as soon as possible. They probably all did. It had been too cold to feel much of anything while they were out in the snow. But as the family started to warm up in the car, it wasn't very long before their clothes all started to burn. Cathy started to wonder if cactus needles were poisonous.

CHAPTER 8
A TRAIL TO NOWHERE

William, Shaun, Chris and Russell were all twenty-five years old and had all been friends for eleven years, since they went to school together. They grew up in a nice town in Ohio and had remained close friends ever since they graduated. As it has a habit of doing, time flew by and they all ended up with jobs and girlfriends, or wives, which then took up the majority of their time. But they always found ways to hang out together as often as they could. They planned to visit the Palm Springs area for a four-day weekend getaway. Russell had a ton of air miles accumulated from his job and he was able to cover everyone's flight.

When the big weekend finally arrived, they each left their jobs a little early that Thursday and met up at Chris' house, where they all jumped into Shaun's car and headed to the airport. The flight to California was as nice as any flight could be. When they arrived at the Palm Springs airport, they found the nighttime desert weather to be quite enjoyable. It was hot. But probably only in the high eighties. There was a nice breeze that left the desert feeling fresh and inviting. The four friends grabbed a taxi to their fancy Palm Springs resort, where they each checked into little cottages and slept for the night.

The weather the following morning wasn't as enjoyable. By

the time all four of them had woken up, got ready and met up in the main yard of the hotel, it was already in the high nineties. But they had come to shop and enjoy the desert town. So they all set out to enjoy the many stores and sites that downtown Palm Springs had to offer. They spent that whole Friday buying random souvenirs and treasures, eating nice big meals and visiting a few different pubs. It wasn't until late after the sun had set that summer night that they decided to call it an evening and returned to their hotel to sleep off the long day of fun.

It was just as hot the following morning. But there was a great big pool at their hotel, complete with a Jacuzzi, a barbecue pit and a nice shady picnic area. So they spent that Saturday lounging around the pool. Shaun and Chris ran out and bought some meat, beer and other foods, which they brought back to the hotel. There was a great deal of barbecuing, a ton of swimming, a little too much sun and way too much beer that day. But they all enjoyed themselves.

As the sun began to set that hot Saturday evening, William started to regret that they hadn't got out of the city much while they were in the desert. When he spoke up to his friends, it appeared that he wasn't alone. Everyone had a great time while they were there. But they hadn't really gone out and done very much. So they all agreed that they would go out the next day and do something that they hadn't done yet on their trip before they had to catch their flight home later that evening. Excited, they all toasted to the new agreement with a cold beer.

A few beers later, Russell had a great idea: they could go hiking! After he told the others his idea and they all agreed it was a great one, they planned out their next day. They would wake early so they could get an early start, they would hike in Whitewater, which was an area not too far from Palm Springs that William had visited on a previous family trip to Palm Springs. Then they would all have a big lunch at the airport and then catch up on some much deserved sleep once they got on the plane. That way they would each be right as rain by the time they got back to Ohio. They were all very excited for the new plans and they all toasted to them with another cold beer.

Chris was the first one to head to his little cottage that night. Russell followed to his own soon after. But William and Shaun stayed up a couple extra hours and enjoyed a few extra drinks before they called it a night. The four of them slept like logs that night. The heat of the summer morning was a rude awakening the following day, as they each awoke to hangovers. It wasn't even 9AM and it must have already been a hundred degrees outside. But they all had agreed to get an early start, so they showed up at the main yard with their luggage before heading to the hotel office to check out.

As Shaun finished checking out first, he then used an app on his cell phone to order them a taxi from the hotel. William finished next and, after remembering how hot it'd been the last time he hiked that area, was smart enough to grab a couple of 2o ounce water bottles that he tucked away into his suitcase. Once everyone had finished checking out of the hotel, they loaded all their luggage into the taxi and headed out for Whitewater. William tried to explain where they wanted to go. It was off Highway 62 and it wasn't the Whitewater Preserve. The driver wasn't exactly sure where they wanted to go, but he turned on the meter and started heading towards Whitewater. The ride wasn't very long, even though the taxi driver drove about eight miles an hour the entire length of the dirt road that they eventually turned onto from the Highway.

They arrived at the place that William had remembered hiking at, a little rectangular dirt parking lot at the end of a long dirt road, shortly after 1oAM. They thanked the taxi driver and tipped him very well for having made him drive to such a remote location and not having an address to begin with. Shaun checked his cell phone to make sure that he had cell service and told the driver that he would be calling for another taxi back to Palm Springs later that afternoon. The driver was kind enough to tell them that they were actually at Mission Creek, not Whitewater, and they should tell the taxi company to pick them up there. They thanked him again as they unloaded their suitcases from the trunk before he turned around and headed back to the city.

The four friends all took in the beautiful summer day. Each hauling a suitcase, they walked around a metal guard rail that kept cars from driving any further down the road and started walking along the trail that followed along where the road ended. There hadn't been anyone else in the little parking lot that they'd been dropped off at and the absolute silence in every direction was a clear indicator that they were totally alone in that beautiful desert land. A bit nervous about being so far off the beaten path, Shaun checked his cell phone again to make sure that he still had service. He had lost one bar of reception, but he still had three left.

Their luggage became too much of a burden for them in no time at all. But they quickly came across a set of stone structures, each furnished only with a picnic table. William took the two 2o ounce bottles of water from his suitcases and tossed one to Chris before the group all tucked their luggage under the picnic table in the structure closest to the trailhead. It was a strange site, but very interesting. The little structures made for some great pictures and a nice hiding spot for their luggage while they hiked. But the group didn't spend very long hanging out there and instead continued walking along the dirt trail. It looked like they were walking down the center of a large valley that would wash out whenever there was a lot of rain in the area.

A little further down the trail they all heard the sound of running water flowing down below the side of the trail where there were too many weeds and dead logs to see source of the noise clearly. The sound of flowing water against the gentle summer breeze had them all curious how much water there actually was down there, so they walked down off the trail to get a closer look. They were a bit disappointed to find that the small creek was little more than a foot across. But, freezing cold as it was, the little stream of desert water did flow rather hard and fast. It was after they had each climbed down off the trail to investigate the stream that they all started to feel a bit sluggish.

They had had all been drinking the night before. They all

got very little sleep and hadn't eaten a breakfast because they were waiting for lunch. But that didn't stop them. It was their last day, it was still early and they had hours left before they had to get back to the airport. William drank his bottle of water in one swift gulp. He then knelt down by the flowing water and refilled the empty water bottle from the cold desert creek. Chris passed his bottle around to Russell and Shaun. When that bottle was empty, Chris refilled it with the cool creek water before the group continued walking down the long dusty trail.

The further back on the trail that they got, the hotter it got all around them. But the beautiful desert valley of rocks and shrubs and the meandering little creek kept their interests sparked. The water didn't last long between the four of them. When the bottles were both empty Chris and William pocketed them. When someone got thirsty next, they'd need to fill up from the little creek. The chilly water along with the gentle breeze that crept through the valley helped them all to beat the summer heat. After some switchbacks where the trail had ascended a bit, Russell suggested that they head down into the creek. While the trail was heading up into nowhere along the foothills, the creek bed below them looked like it stayed pretty level.

It didn't take much convincing for the group to break from the trail and head off down the creek bed. Much to their surprise, the running water had completely diverted, or they were turned around. Because after they descended to the creek bed and started walking, they weren't able to locate any running water. It wasn't a big deal, as none of them were thirsty. But they would have refilled their bottles earlier if they had known there wasn't going to be water down there with them. The valley they hiked through was wide and looked like it went on for miles. This was exactly how they had wanted to spend their last day.

By 1PM in the afternoon, they hadn't stopped traveling along the dry creek bed, but they still hadn't found more water. From what they could see ahead, it looked like the valley wrapped around to a very green looking area. Trekking along the sandy creek bed wasn't quite as easy as walking the trail had been and the sun was beating down harder than it had all day. However, this didn't detour them and the lush green sight ahead kept the group moving forward. It wasn't until they reached the bend in the valley that they could see just how green the area really was. Even though it was well into summer, the area they found themselves in was covered in green foliage as far as they could see, complete with grassy hills that were adorned with little white, yellow and purple flowers.

The site was beautiful and all four of them started off in different directions to admire different parts of the green valley they found themselves in. No one got too far from each other, but it was easy to see that the green valley continued to wrap around and probably met up with the creek bed that they had hiked on to get there and then needed to return through. After everyone had taken pictures and had frolicked around like they'd never seen wild grass before, the group continued along the curving green valley where they planned to catch up to the large creek bed that they'd taken to get there. Then they would head back and get some food, because they were all starting to get very hungry.

Following along the curve in the green valley, their stomachs each started to churn just a bit. They'd had enjoyed a ton of beers the night before, but hadn't exactly pigged out on barbecue. After trekking along for a bit longer, it was William who's stomach first started to do more than churn. In no time at all, William went from a healthy hiker to a sweaty, messy walker. Something didn't feel right with his stomach and his three friends could clearly see the color draining from his sweaty face when he began to complain that he didn't feel well. By that point, they had reached what looked like the dry, sandy wash that they had taken to get there. They turned onto the water torn creek bed and began rushing towards the trailhead.

It wasn't much of a rush, as they all waited along for William to keep up. Chris had propped William's arm over his shoulder and was helping his sickly friend through the sand. Shaun tried to call their taxi ahead of time, hoping to have it arrive at the trailhead before they did. But somewhere along the hike he had completely lost reception. Indeed, everyone's cell phone had lost reception. Even more unfortunate for them all was the fact that the dry creek bed that they hiked along was not the one that they'd taken to get to the green valley. But they didn't realize that for the better part of an hour. By then, it was nearly 3PM in the afternoon and they all knew they needed to get back to the trailhead as soon as possible.

Shaun hadn't found any reception, but kept his phone handy, ever hopeful that they would find service. If he did, he'd call for emergency help, because William's face had turned pale and he was getting slower and slower with each step they took. But they'd just as soon find a taxi in the middle of that creek bed than they would cellular service. When they decided to turn around and head back through the green valley that they'd come through, fear really hit them all. Everything in the opposite direction looked green and lush. Every valley that branched off from the creek bed they were now walking along was filled with grass and flowers. They didn't slow down, but tried to be extra observant of their surroundings as they wanted to make sure that they returned through the original green twisting valley that they'd first come through.

When they came across the area that they thought they'd entered the second dry creek bed from, they made the turn and hurried along through the green valley that looked like each of the other ones they'd seen in the last couple of hours. By this time, all of their stomachs were beginning to feel sour and they each slowed down a great deal. The sun beat down on top of them harder and harder as they walked along. The beautiful green valley that they had been so fond of now appeared like a green death trap to the group as they trekked along as best as they could.

By the time they reached they end of the green valley and found themselves at the face of a familiar looking grand sized valley and dry creed bed, the sun had taken its toll on each of them. The green valley offered a little afternoon shade and a cool breeze which comforted them all, while the creek bed offered no shade and looked hot and exhausting. The four sickly friends decided to rest there at the face of the valley for a while. They would gather a little strength and then get to the trailhead, and more importantly, cell service, as soon as they possibly could. Shaun checked his cell phone one more time, only to find no reception and a dying phone battery.

After sitting down in the shade and resting their exhausted feet, all four of the dehydrated men quickly fell asleep. It wasn't until the sun had set behind a tall mountain in the distance and a cold breeze had crept through the grassy valley where they slept, that William woke up in a feverish chill. He didn't say a word, nor did he take any time to wake his three friends. In a dehydration induced belligerence and a fever induced panic, William simple walked off through the dry creek bed towards a destination unknown.

Chris woke next, in a cold sweat. Though he felt horrible, he quickly came to his senses and woke Shaun and Russell. The three of them all knew that they were in a lot of trouble. They were cold, the sun was completely set by now and from what they could gather, William's footprints trailed off into the dry creed bed headed in the opposite direction of the trailhead. The three dehydrated men knew they needed to get to the trailhead where their cell phones would work and they could call for help. They also needed to find their friend, William. As the cold breeze swept past each of them, they headed into the sandy creek bed and disappeared into the dark summer night.

When they missed their flight that day, the airline didn't send a rescue team to locate them. No one from their hotel went looking for them. The taxi company didn't get a second call from them that afternoon. But that didn't raise any red flags and the taxi company never thought twice about it. All four of their cell phones died before they were able to get to any place that had cellular service.

But the following day, a kind and concerned couple who were headed out on a hike of their own, found four suitcases under a picnic table at the trailhead. When the suitcases were still there after they returned from their hike, the couple reported it to the authorities who began searching for the four young tourists. They eventually found all four of them together in the dry creek bed. Unfortunately, they found them all far too late to help any of them.

CHAPTER 9
SPOILING THE LOCALS

Sam and Ruth had known Kurt and Daisy for almost thirty years. They'd all attended college together before Sam and Kurt started working for the same advertising firm in Seattle, WA. Each of them were almost at the age where they could comfortably retire. But they all still kept up full-time jobs. In fact, they all worked way too much and really wanted few days off to just relax. When winter fleeted and the weather started getting nicer, they jumped on the Internet and visited an online rental service. There they booked a week-long stay in a pair of little cabins next door to each other in the High Desert area of Southern California.

When the morning came for them to take their week off, both couples were ecstatic as they met up at the airport. They parked both of their cars in an extended-stay parking lot and started making their way towards checking their baggage. The rental they had booked was advertised as being "pet friendly," so Daisy had brought along her dog, a little Sheltie named Walter who had a massive coat and an even bigger personality. Walter had to get into a crate that they wheeled along with their suitcases. Sam and Ruth were sad they hadn't brought their dogs along for the trip. But their son always watched their animals when they went on vacation.

They checked all their luggage, including Walter, and boarded a plane that took them down the west coast to Palm Springs, CA. After retrieving their luggage and a very upset and lonely Walter, they rented a big SUV that could fit all of them and headed up the highway to the High Desert. They loved how the desert looked and took pictures all along the drive. They went through a small city and then passed along a beautiful rocky road before passing through a little place named Pioneertown and on into the mountains. They found the entrance to their private little rentals down a long dirt road in Burns Canyon. It looked like it was exactly what they had wanted: small, beautiful and acres from any other residence.

Standing alone in the middle of a Joshua Tree and rock filled desert were two little stone cabins with a handful of other little structures around them, all fenced in behind a big chink link fence. After retrieving a hidden key from underneath an interesting looking mailbox, Kurt unlocked a big gate before Sam drove the SUV inside and up to the stone cabins. Kurt locked up the gate behind them before they let Walter out of the car. Antsy from the traveling and curious about where they were, the fluffy dog bolted out of the car and ran through the property like a lightning bolt, barking and smelling everything in sight.

The front of each stone cabin opened towards one another and in between them was a big and shady tree-lined courtyard with picnic tables, lounge chairs and a huge stone barbecue right in the center. Each couple picked a side and began unloading their luggage into their cabins while Walter ran back and forth over the courtyard, investigating everything he could see and smell. Each cabin had a little kitchenette, a big bed, a small bathroom, a smaller closet and a back door that lead to little private patios which backed up against the property's fence. It really was exactly what they had all wanted and, indeed, needed.

No one wasted any time taking advantage of the beautiful grounds. Sam and Ruth took advantage of the lounge chairs in the courtyard, kicked their feet up and took in the afternoon desert view from a shady spot. Kurt and Daisy walked around the chin link fence that bordered the property with their dog, making sure that there wasn't anywhere that he could get through. After settling in for a while, the four of them felt right at home. They spent the first few days having a bunch of good old fashioned fun at those cabins. They'd go out for a big dinner down in Yucca Valley and then bring back a bunch of food a supplies so they could stay the rest of each day at their cabins and enjoy themselves in privacy.

There were miles of hiking trails right there by the little cabins which they all started exploring after a few days of lounging around the rentals. Daisy brought Walter along the first day that they all decided to hike a nearby trail and the city raised dog had a blast. So the next day, naturally, Kurt and Daisy didn't think twice about taking Walter along when both couples wanted to hike another trail that went off in a different direction over a couple of short ridges and up into the mountains. This hike proved to be just as fun as the first one and twice as beautiful. After getting over those two short ridges, the path wound up through some beautiful boulders as it wrapped around the side of a mountain. Unfortunately, the trail started to climb up in altitude and soon wore every one of them out. Everyone except Walter, that was.

They spent that warm evening in the courtyard while Kurt barbecued a bunch of fancy burgers and sausages they had picked up from a market when they'd gone to dinner the night before. The courtyard between the two cabins turned out to be the spot where they all hung out the most. Both couples had spent a little time enjoying their little private patios late each night around bedtime. But the majority of their vacation had been spent enjoying their time together, and their time together had mainly been spent enjoying that shady courtyard. That night proved no exception, when they barbecued for over a straight hour before they each enjoyed multiple burgers and sausages.

Later that night they all sat around the picnic tables and finished their last plates of food. Kurt offered everyone some

69

more, but the group was already filled to their max. As he bagged some trash and cleared most of the table, all that was eventually left was a tray filled with sausages and a stack of burgers half a foot tall. No one was surprised when Kurt gave Daisy's dog a burger when she took the sleepy pup to their cabin to sleep. But afterwards, when Kurt randomly picked up a few of the sausages with a serving fork and flung them over the fence while he was taking the tray into their cabin, it caught Sam and Ruth by surprise.

When Kurt and Daisy returned to the courtyard, Sam and Ruth were very curious and asked Kurt why he'd thrown the meat over the fence. Sam and Ruth were a bit shocked to learn that Kurt and Daisy had been tossing all their leftovers over the fence behind their cabin each night. Kurt explained that he and Daisy normally gave their dog most of their leftovers, but as they'd had so much from being on vacation, they had been tossing a bunch out for other animals. Daisy was a stickler for letting food spoil and there was no way that they would have been able to eat all of that barbecue before it went bad. As odd as it had appeared, Kurt explained it well enough and the topic of discussion soon turned to something they had all been dreading.

Their vacation had been a blast so far. But it was quickly coming to an end. Sam, Ruth, Kurt and Daisy only had two more days left at their desert getaway. But that second day wasn't going to be much fun, as they needed to wake up early, checkout and then catch a flight back home that left early in the afternoon. So before they all went to bed that night, they came up with a plan for the next day. The following morning, everyone woke up early and enjoyed a nice breakfast together in the shady courtyard before heading out to get a full day of desert fun. They packed up some extra water and a plentiful picnic meal into Sam's backpack before they grabbed Walter and headed to the second, more scenic, mountain trail that they had all enjoyed the day before.

After they passed over the two small ridges, climbing up the rocky trail proved to be just as grueling as it had the first time. But the beautiful desert scenery, the extra water and the fact that it was their last day kept everyone moving along. Walter didn't need any extra motivation and basically dragged Daisy all the way. Shortly after noon, near the top of the mountain, they found a nice flat spot along the trail that was shaded from the hot sun by a large boulder which also blocked the steady breeze that swept across the mountain side. Sam pulled out the picnic meal and a bottle of water for everyone and they ate a large and delicious meal while enjoying the wonderful desert scenery.

Everyone ate their portion of the food before Kurt and Daisy cleaned everything up while Sam and Ruth took pictures of the bright clouds above and the breezy desert below. Once Kurt was finished packing up the remains of the picnic, he walked over to Sam and handed him his backpack. Daisy took Walter's leash and everyone returned to hiking up the trail. It wasn't twenty more minutes before they reached the top of the mountain. The sight from that vantage point was truly amazing. But up there, the soft breeze they'd all felt below had turned into a heavy wind.

They posed for a few pictures together while the midday sun stretched out across the vast landscape of boulders and Joshua Trees below them. But the nonstop heavy wind whipped across the mountaintop so fast that it was hard for everyone to hear one another even when they were standing right next to each other. They had had a great day and a truly wonderful vacation. But the whipping desert winds seemed to be a force that pushed them towards the inevitable end of their trip. Slowly, they all started back down the trail towards their little cabins.

Walter hadn't slowed down a bit that day and had used his leash to pull Daisy along the entire time. When the tired group neared the bottom of the mountain, Daisy stopped, made Walter sit and then unhooked his leash. She gave the dog a handful of orders and then continued on along with everyone else. It had been a much harder hike than any one of them had expected and Daisy was just about exhausted. Kurt offered to walk the dog on his leash for Daisy, but she insisted that Walter was very well trained and that they weren't very far from the cabins.

It appeared that Walter was in fact very well behaved, as he kept to Daisy's side while they all continued walking down the trail. The wind was long gone, far above them, and it seemed as if the breeze had died down too. As they walked along, the only thing they could hear around them was the sound of birds chirping and the jingle of Walter's leash as he trotted along beside them. But when they finally neared the bottom of the hill, the obedient dog began barking down the trail ahead of them. When Daisy went to scold him, Walter took off and ran down the trail.

They all called out to him, but the dog didn't look back for a second as he ran down the mountainside. Everyone was exhausted from the long day, but sluggishly started jogging down the trail after him as Daisy continued to yell out his name. It was clear that they weren't making any real difference by jogging, so the four of them stopped for a second and caught their breath. Daisy was concerned, but noted that they weren't far from the cabins and Walter had probably seen them up ahead. Hoping that they'd find him at the rental or someone along the way, they continued along down the trail.

Far out of their sight, at the bottom of the mountain, Walter followed a scent that had his hormones going wild. The scent grew stronger as he wondered up and over the first ridge following the trail further towards the little cabins. But there, along trail at the bottom of a shallow valley, he slowed down and paused in his tracks. As he curiously sniffed out that scent in the air, Walter noticed a small coyote standing further up the valley, right before it twisted out of view. Just the scent of that wild animal drove the domesticated dog's hormones crazy and Walter instantly ran off the trail and up the valley towards it.

Seeing the dog give chase, the coyote turned around and ran up the twisting valley until it was out of view. Walter chased quickly behind it, until he too followed along where the valley turned. Just as the curious dog rounded the corner, four other coyotes crept out of hiding from along the ridge and quickly ran after poor Walter. Daisy and everyone else passed over the two short ridges just moments later. But unfortunately, none of them were there soon enough to see where Walter went, or the band of wild animals that had followed him. When everyone reached the cabins shortly after that, their dog wasn't there.

Everyone then went back out and looked for Walter for the rest of that day. Then they even ended up stayed at the cabins for an extra two days, hoping all the while that they would find their little friend. But there wasn't any trace of him and, sadly, no one ever saw Walter again. Those coyotes had been attracted to that area when they kept finding food there. They all knew exactly what to do when they found Walter alone. Being a domesticated dog, the poor guy stood no chance against them.

Those four hikers returned soon home a bit gloomy. And, even though they had all truly loved their accommodations, a heartbroken Daisy soon left a depressing and far from positive online review with the rental service they had used for the little pet friendly stone cabins.

CHAPTER 10
"WE'LL COME BACK FOR YOU!"

Joel, Kevin and Bill had all been best friends since they met as little kids growing up in Wisconsin. They had done plenty of growing up and were all now pushing forty years old. They all came from wealthy families and had all finished college in their early twenties before taking on professional careers. After a decade and a half, they had each grown tired of their careers and retired. Neither of them really needed to worry about money and they all had a passion for traveling. So they retired early together and started traveling the world.

One cool spring day, the three of them met up in Joshua Tree, CA. They had rented a house near the National Park, where they all met up with each other and planned to stay there until it got too hot for their taste. The house was huge and included a theater room, pool, a Jacuzzi, tennis courts and it backed up against BLM land, which offered total privacy, endless hiking trails and lots of off roading access. They stayed close to home for the first few days. The pool and theater room saw most of their attention, followed by the barbecue and finally, their beds.

During those first few days, they didn't really do much with their time. They all slept-in each morning, watched movies and barbecued by the pool while enjoying a hefty supply of beer.

75

But eventually they started making their way out of the house and into the desert around them. They enjoyed Joshua Tree National Park, but they liked going out to Twentynine Palms, Landers or Johnson Valley even more. There, they could ride the fancy truck that Kevin had rented and the four-wheel ATVs each of them had rented, just about anywhere. Plus, there they were able to enjoy plenty of privacy in the vast and beautiful desert while doing so.

Johnson Valley became their favorite spot, as it wasn't host to numerous tourists attractions, like Joshua Tree, Pioneertown and Landers were. Sure, all three of them enjoyed all of those places too. Sure, there was barbecue in a few of those spots that would easily knock your socks off. But in Johnson Valley, they were able to ride all day long without seeing much more than a handful of other off-roading motorists and open dirt trails ahead of them.

By their second month in the High Desert, Joel, Kevin and Bill had all grown a heavy addiction for driving through the endless sandy hills around them as fast as their wheels could take them. They also enjoyed exploring the desert and developed a habit of having a good old fashioned picnic in the middle of nowhere most days, simply because they liked eating somewhere they'd never been before. Riding in one direction as long as they could before they all decided it was time to stop and eat was their idea of heaven and they loved every minute they spent under the desert sun doing it.

It wasn't long before they stumbled across one of the desert's many abandon mining operations while riding aimlessly through Johnson Valley. When they saw what looked like a cement building off in the foothills ahead of them, they went to get a closer view of what random site stood in the middle of nowhere. Upon further investigation, they found a pair of dilapidated brick buildings, a few crumbling cement foundations and an old mine shaft. The shaft had been filled in with cement and the buildings were in shambles. But Joel, Kevin and Bill were each ecstatic as they all parked their four-wheelers and walked around the area.

They spent the better part of the day hanging out and exploring that site. It was Kevin who ended up doing some online research later that evening and what he found further excited all three of them. The area was home to tons of old mining operations, many of which had been abandon a long time ago. The BLM had closed the entrances or limited access to them years back. But there were a bunch of old sites they could go check out in the area that they already loved so much. Kevin wrote down the coordinates to a handful of sites and plugged them into his GPS and the next few days were all spent on their ATVs or in that big fancy truck, exploring some of the many deserted mining sites near Johnson Valley.

One day they all ventured out together in Kevin's big truck so they could check out some areas north of Johnson Valley that were truly high up and hard to reach in any vehicle. They headed up a narrow dirt road, covered on both sides with large boulders, that turned back and forth as it winded its way up the steep incline of a mountainside. At the top of tall and narrow ridge half way up the mountain, the road wound along shortly, before descending over the other side into a valley the three of them had never seen before. Once they had descended the switchbacks on the other side of that tall ridge, they explored the new area. It wasn't until later that afternoon that they stumbled across an old abandoned site at the face of a steep hill.

To their surprise, this was a site that they hadn't seen on the internet or any of the maps that they'd purchased. Now, there must have been a million old mining operations in the area. So the discovery of the undocumented site didn't really come as any surprise to them. The BLM had also come through and restricted access to the majority of the mine shafts in the area by filling vertical shafts in with cement or installing large metal barriers at the front of horizontal shafts. So the newer looking metal frame at the entrance to what looked like a cave at the foot of that steep hill didn't really surprise any of them any. What did surprise them, was the fact that they found the thick metal pillars that had once barred entrance to that cave cut through and bent out of place.

It looked as if someone had used something like a welding torch to cut through the top of most of the bars before bending them down and off too the side sometime after the BLM had installed the metal barrier. That left a narrow hole between a bunch of rusty, twisted metal bars, which looked easy enough for someone to climb over. The three of them stood near the face of the cave in awe. They had seen plenty of different types of mining sites in the area. But this was the first one that they'd found which they might actually get to explore. They wasted no time. Kevin used his key fob to lock the truck behind them and they went about entering the cave.

Kevin was the first one to climb over the rusty bent bars and into the entrance of the dark cave. "It's so dark in here!" he yelled out to his friends as soon as he was on the other side.

Bill climbed over the rusty bars next and Joel followed quickly afterwards.

"It's cold in here!" Joel said as soon as he jumped over the bars. "Holy cow! It is dark. But it is really cold!"

Bill's observation was all but ignored as each of them grabbed their cell phones from their pockets and flicked them on to create some much needed light. As soon as they had their phones on, they were walking into the impressive, but incredibly dark, rock cave. It must have been ten feet tall and was probably a dozen feet wide. It smelled like an unfinished basement and, to Bill's credit, it was at least ten degrees colder that it had been outside. The further they got from the cave's entrance, the more the glow from their cell phones helped light up the dark and musty cave. Slowly, the light from the entrance dimmed lower and lower, until a slight curve in the cave's direction all but cut off the small glow of natural light all together.

This wasn't a problem for them, as their cell phones were bright as flashlights and clearly lit up the amazing underground environment around them. Big wooden beams were anchored to the sides of the rock walls every ten to twelve feet or so, and in places along the ceiling, long boards were laid from beam to beam. Likely in areas that were more prone to caving in. The wood looked like it had to of been over a hundred years old, but appeared to be just as solid as the rock that it covered.

It wasn't long before they came upon round chamber that had three additional and seemingly identical tunnels branching off of it. There was one tunnel to the right, one straight ahead and a final tunnel to the left. The round chamber itself must have been twenty feet in diameter and amazed all three of them. From that underground site, one could easily see the vast differences in the minerals that composed the heart of the mountain that they were walking inside. The tunnel they had entered from was composed of a dark rock, as was the tunnel that ran parallel with it. But the tunnels that branched off in perpendicular directions were more of a shiny white, milky looking rock.

Their cell phone batteries had already started to wear down, but this was a magical place and they had hardly explored as much as they wanted to. One by one, they checked out the tunnels, heading into the one on their left first. That milky white tunnel ended after about a hundred feet, where it appeared that the dark rock had started getting heavier. Exiting that short little excavation, they headed down the dark rock tunnel on their left. This tunnel proved to be even shorter than the previous one as they'd only traveled maybe fifty feet in, before the black rock walls narrowed until it wasn't a tunnel anymore.

The third tunnel they entered from the round chamber, again to their left, was the ticket. In big sections on both sides, the walls seemed like they were made entirely out of a shiny white, crystal looking material. After traveling down the beautiful looking tunnel, they arrived at another fork in the cave. Joel was eager to check out both branches, but Bill and Kevin were both very hesitant. They each had about thirty to forty percent of battery life left on their cell phones and the light from those phones was the only way they could get out of the cave. Additionally, Kevin noted that the sun had been starting to set when they'd entered the cave and they had wanted to travel back to the paved roads before it got too dark out.

To this, Joel suggested a simple solution. He would go and check out one of the tunnels real quick, to appease his curiosity, while they could both wait there at the fork in the tunnel, where they could use just one cell phone and save a little power as Joel explored just a little bit more. This worked for everyone, so Joel headed off into the tunnel on the right, through an equally beautiful white crystal cave where he followed it along until it veered off to the left and he went out of sight. Kevin pocketed his cell phone after he tried to take a couple pictures of the interesting shiny white crystal clusters that surrounded them.

Just a few minutes later, a small dim light blinked and swayed into sight far ahead of them, maybe two hundred feet away. The light was just bright enough to illuminate the silhouette of a person staggering towards them. However, this figure was walking towards them from the tunnel to their left. They weren't at all startled, as, after all, there couldn't be too many people down there lighting their path with a cell phone. Joel had veered off to the left when he'd gone out of sight. So the fork must have actually been the head of a loop in the cave. Kevin and Bill both watched the light bump up and down over the rocky floor as the partially illuminated figure grew closer and closer. But in an instant, the light fell straight down and out of sight. This was accompanied by the loud echo of a scream which was instantly cut short and then the grinding clatter of rocks tumbling.

Bill immediately gave chase into the tunnel which still echoed with the sound of rumbling. Kevin grabbed for his cell phone for some light and hurried to catch up with Bill. As they neared the site of the commotion in an instant, Kevin and Bill were both able to spot the face of a wide hole in the center of the tunnel. As they cautiously approached it and looked down, they were both horrified to see that the vertical shaft went some two or three stories down. The same dim light that they'd seen illuminating Joel just seconds earlier, now lit a horrific scene many feet below. Joel laid there, twisted and sprawled out on the rocky floor below, with the phone still somehow in

80

or at least near his hand.

As their eyes were able to focus with the poor aid of their dim cell phones, a chill simultaneously ran through both Kevin and Bill which left them cold as ice. As they turned to each other in disbelief, the shock in their eyes was suddenly interrupted by a low gargle from below.

"I... need help." they heard Joel say from far down below; his tone so stressed and desperate that it truly sounded painful for him to say. The twisted mass that was their friend began to move ever so slowly just as the light from his phone went off.

"Joel! Can you move?" yelled out a panicked Kevin.

There was a long pause as Bill and Kevin both hurriedly tried to extend the light from their phones as deep down into the cave as they could without falling down themselves. Seconds later, the light from Joel's cell phone turned back on.

"I can move." Joel painfully moaned up the shaft. "But I think I broke my legs. I need help!" he said as his voice instantly turned from confused and pain-ridden to panicked and desperate.

"We're going to get you out of there, buddy!" Bill yelled. "Just relax."

"Can you breathe okay?" asked Kevin, trying not to sound as panicked as he actually was.

There was another long pause from the dimly lit figure before Joel responded. "I can breathe okay. But I need help. Please get me help!" Joel whimpered.

"Just hold tight, man! We're going to go get you help right now!" yelled Bill.

This time there wasn't much of a pause. "I'm really cold and I'm hurt really bad." moaned Joel. "My phone is dying. Please don't let me be stuck down here in the dark." he cried up to them.

"Don't worry!" yelled Kevin. "We're going right now!"

Kevin turned around and hastily headed back from where they'd all come in.

"We're going to get you out of there in no time!" Bill yelled down. "We'll come back for you!"

With that, Bill turned away from his crying friend deep below and cautiously hurried back to the cave's entrance along with Kevin. The sounds of them shuffling and breathing heavily echoed all around them as they ran along with their phone lights aimed towards the ground in front of them. They made it back to the dimly lit entrance in very little time. Bill jumped over the rusty bent metal bars and out into the hot desert with ease. But Kevin slipped as he was clearing the entrance and he toppled over onto the other side letting out a curse as he landed.

The sun had already began to set in the valley around them as they exited the cave. Kevin had twisted his right ankle and was instantly in pain. But a determined Bill quickly grabbed him, thew Kevin's arm over his shoulders and started supporting him to the truck. While propping Kevin along, Bill tried to dial 911 on his cell phone. But they were just about as far from away from cell phone reception as one can get in California. They needed to get Joel help as soon as they possibly could. So Kevin limped over to the passenger's side of his truck and tossed Bill the keys.

They were in the truck and tearing up the road in a flash, ascending the dirt switchbacks like they were a paved race course. Kevin took out his GPS and made an indication of where the entrance to the cave was while Bill raced towards the top of the ridge. As Bill neared the top of the tall and narrow ridge that they'd gone over on the way there, Kevin tried his cell phone to no avail. The sun had cast long shadows over the valley where they'd entered the cave. But as they got closer and closer to the top of the ridge, the still shining light from the setting sun got brighter and brighter.

Bill hastily grabbed his phone once again, this time just hoping to see maybe one or two bars of cell service, as they'd already almost driven out of that valley. Bill only focused on his cell phone screen for a split second. Just long enough to see that he still didn't have any service before he tossed it into his lap. Just as he did so, the truck tore up to the very top of the tall and narrow ridge, where the last of the sun's bright and blinding beams of light still shined. The bright orange sun hit Bill's eyes just hard enough for him to close them and as he did so, the dirt road ahead of them sharply turned to the right. Bill, blinded for just a brief moment, wasn't able to make that sharp turn as quickly as he had made the previous turns.

As a result, the truck flew up the ridge and directly over the other side where Bill quickly lost control of it. The truck and it's two passengers were rolled over and over, harder and harder, until the battered truck finally came to an abrupt stop, upside-down, when it hit one of the large granite boulders the peppered the landscape. While an injured and delirious Bill and Kevin hung upside-down, strapped to their seats by their seat-belts, they both drifted in and out of consciousness. It was clear that they were now going to need just as much help as Joel did. But they were both too injured to do much of anything and both fell unconscious.

After the sun set, a cold breeze began to blow over the desert that night. After some time, Kevin was suddenly awoken to a great deal of pain and discomfort when his cell phone flashed on. It had landed on the cracked windshield which was just below him and it vibrated as it flashed on just inches from his head, which temporarily woke him from his injured daze. The last thing that Kevin was able to see was his cell phone flashing and buzzing to show that it's battery was at just 1% and it was going to turn off while an unresponsive Bill hung upside down beside him.

As Kevin focused through his pain, he clearly saw that his cell phone also showed that he had five out of five possible bars of cellular service. When that fuzzy and fatally ironic fact clicked in his head, Kevin's phone vibrated one more time and turned itself off just as he slowly fell back unconscious. As Joel laid broken and dying at the bottom of a dark mine shaft that night, Kevin and Bill laid upside-down in a truck, each strapped into their car seats and dying. However, albeit a small consolation, it was the batteries in their cell phones that died before they all did.

Keep An Eye Out For

88.6% of the People Who Visit the Morongo Basin
Are 1oo% Idiots

Volume II

Made in the USA
Monee, IL
10 June 2023

35466279R00056